Jack Be Nimble

A novella
Written by S. G. Lee
Copyright 2017 © Sheilagh G. Lee
E-Book Edition 2016

SB

An imprint of Shillelagh Books
London, Ontario, Canada

Acknowledgments:
Sincere thanks to Jodi and Sydney, without your constant support and encouragement, this book would not be possible. You are the best friends a writer could have. I dedicate this book to my daughters, my son-in law and my husband; who have supported my writing endeavours with encouragement and love. Special thanks to my beloved mother in heaven, who taught me dreams, can come true with hard work, perseverance and patience.

Table of Contents

Preface: A Note from the Teller of Tales

Have you ever fell in love; even though you thought you never would? Fate plays weird tricks. Read about my how I met and won the love of my life, Patty and how that love was almost lost forever, not once but three times.

Jack

Sucker

I t all started Monday morning and boy, I hated Monday

mornings. As I climbed the steps to my tiny office, I could feel the waves of heat; already seeping through my cheap suit. It was hot enough to fry an egg out there and it was only eight a.m. The door was stiff in the heat and I noted that someone had tried to break in. There were scratches by the door. Everything looked in its place. The cabinet with my files was still locked as was my desk, obviously an attempt to break in, but not a success on their behalf. My half- empty bottle of cheap hooch was still there.

I threw my hat up on the coat rack in the corner and peeled off my suit coat jacket hoping that my window fan would kick in soon. Then I took the bag, I carried with my breakfast, over to the coffee cup on the shelf. I cracked the two eggs into it and then poured orange juice over them. Oops, almost forgot the chaser a little Tabasco sauce. Good for what ailed me, as my head ached from the cocktails I'd imbibed last night. I then sat in my desk chair, blessing the fact that I had been gifted by a client with a chair which had swivel wheels. I swiveled for a bit, then turned and faced my door; wishing for a client to breeze in to end my boredom.

I read my etched name Jack Daniel Forbes private investigator, on the door for the fifteenth time. I twirled in my chair once again, to look at it and found a woman standing there. And not just any woman, this woman was a knock-out. She had blonde hair in fashionable chignon. A real looker with her bright blue eyes and come hither smile, and gams that want on and on. Her skirt was split up to the knee. She had the look of that movie star... you know the one I mean. Carol Lombard now she was classy, not like that Mae West who you couldn't bring home to your mother. Except the dame wasn't smiling, but grimacing, as if to keep from crying. As she pulled out a tear stained handkerchief and walked over closer to me; I could see her eyes were red and puffy as well.

"Are you Mr. Forbes?" she asked her voice musical even when trembling.

"Yah, I'm Jack Daniel Forbes like the sign says," I answered, intrigued by whatever she wants to tell me.

"Can I trust you?" she asked.

"I'm very trustworthy ma'am, unless you've committed a crime, there are no worries on that score," I reassured her.

"I have to trust someone. I'm going out of my mind," she stated hesitating "Maybe if I knew a little bit more about you?"

"Well you know the skinny on me. My name is Jack Daniel Forbes. I was copper for ten years, until the heat got a little too hot when I turned in some flatfeet, for being on the take. That old blue wall went up and this detective was down for the count, until I opened up my own private investigation office three years ago."

"That's all very interesting I suppose, but I still don't know that I should trust you. If word should get back...."

"I was named after the whiskey bottle my mother finished the night I was conceived. Hey why do I tell you that? That's a little bit too personal sorry." I blurted out knowing that I was lying but hey I couldn't help myself. Didn't I tell you she was a looker? She looked at me like I Had two heads

Surprising myself I continued making an effort. I felt that I fumbled a little there something about this dame made me want to reveal everything about myself, to her. Of course I did the dance, a little charm and schmooze that I was famous for and I felt she'd be putty in my hands. She wasn't. She seemed immune to my charisma.

I rarely brought up my childhood even to lie about it. What had I been thinking? I had been a cop for ten years and I did turn in a flatfoot on the take break the code of blue; but I had escaped my criminal childhood years before that. My real moniker was Giovanni Fabbrizzo Junior, better known as little Johnny or Jack Giovanni in the neighborhood where I grown up and I used to run numbers for my daddy's best friend. Until I had my ears boxed. Wait a minute; forget what I said and forget you heard that name, I'm Jack Daniel Forbes now that's my moniker and don't forget it.

"No, I appreciate your candor; I'm not much for banter anyway. I suppose I can reveal things about myself as well. My name is Mrs. Grace-Ellen Parks and someone is trying to kill me," she blurted out and then began sobbing all over the place.

Now am I sucker when a women cries. I can't stand the wallowing. It does something to me. My insides turn to Jell-O and all I want to do was take her in my arms, but she said she was a Mrs., and I respect the bonds of matrimony. So I just patted her arm saying there, there and handed her the handkerchief out of my suit coat jacket.

"You are a gentleman, aren't you?" she said glancing at me in surprise and wiping her eyes gently patting them.

"I try ma'am, "I replied thinking she had all the ear markings of a vulnerable woman that I could sashay into my bed when this had been wrapped up.

"My husband is trying to kill me!" she stated, in a stage whisper as if she was afraid to say it.

"No, you have to be mistaken. He'd have to be crazy to get rid of a knock-out of a broad like you," I replied.

"I am not mistaken. Maybe you weren't the right man for the job after all," she exclaimed rising in a graceful way.

"No wait, Mrs. Grace-Ellen Parks. If your ball and chain really tried to do away with you, then you need someone like me to prevent it."

"I don't know what to do what if I'm wrong? I wouldn't want it getting back to my ex-husband," she retorted.

"Ex, but you just said he was your husband." I protested.

"A slip of the tongue, he divorced me a few months ago, but my Daddy, Judge Banks got me alimony. I'm not poor, I can pay your fee," she explained.

"Oh, so that's it, your ex wants to rid himself of you to stop letting out his pockets. We can fix that."

"Do you think that's it?" she asked excited.

"Yes," I replied proudly.
"Come to my house at six p.m. so we can plan some more. Here's the address. Don't be late," she demanded then added with a kiss she blew at me, "Goodbye, Sir Launcelot."

I stewed most of the afternoon wondering what she expected me to do at six p.m. Am I just the muscle to her? I'm not in the business just to be a fathead. That's the way a guy gets hurt or possibly killed in this job.. But the dame needed help as long as he wasn't a trigger man I was safe. But just to be safe I'd bring my shooter.

At five twenty five p.m. I went to my desk drawer to get my gun a Remington .41 caliber Double Derringer. My only purchase when becoming a private detective, this baby was my pride and joy. I had my throw away strapped to my ankle calf. It would certainly defend the dame from her murderous ex. I turned the key and to my surprise no gun. Damn someone had gotten in here after all and they had my gun. Why hadn't I noticed its absence earlier? I would have to report it missing later to some of my buddies, ones I still had left on the force. I'd be late if I didn't hurry. Thank goodness I had my trusty back-up. It wasn't as nice or even as accurate in my opinion, but it would do in a pinch.

I arrived at the address a few minutes before six p.m. to see the door a jar. Had he gotten in ahead of me? I bounded up the stairs to hear a gunshot. Was I too late? I ran into the house hoping to find her and save her. I heard yet another gunshot coming from the upstairs bedroom. I bounded up the stairs, opened the door, to find her holding the gun over a man bloodied on the floor. He had a huge wound in his chest, he bled heavily from. She had shot him straight through the forehead the second time. That was not a pretty picture, as the blow back disgusted me to say the least. She stood frozen as if in shock and then the shivering began. I went to the bedroom next door and grabbed a blanket, throwing it around her shoulders. Poor woman! She'd defended herself and this was the result; then I noticed my missing gun lying beside his body.

"He tried to kill me. I shot him," she croaked.

"Yah, you're all wet, muffin. You took my shooter and you plugged him Clearly it was premeditated," I complained loudly.

"I had to, I was so scared," she answered, tears pooling in her eyes again,

What could a man do? I could only stand those tears so long; I took her in my arms and comforted her, only to have her push me into the bedroom next door. I let matters get out of hand and the next thing I know the cops break in, guns a blaze to find us in flagrante delicto. She's crying rape and saying I killed her husband. She's shaking like a leaf and they're buying her every word. I was toast. You look at me and you look at her and who would you believe?

We were both arrested her sticking to her story that I killed her husband and had tried to rape her. (Yes he was her husband, not her ex as she claimed.) She claimed I stalked her and her husband had spoken severely to me. Then I had plotted to kill him to have her.

It seemed I was in a fix. I used my one phone call to reach out to my buddy on the force, Pat O'Malley. I hadn't seen Pat in a few years, but Pat was eager to prove that Grace-Ellen was a fraud and a murderess.

I was in jail nearly a week, before the key came to breaking Grace-Ellen's story came out. I stored the gun in my desk drawer but the bullets? The bullets were stored in my room under the floorboards. Grace-Ellen had to buy bullets so she could plug her husband. Pat O'Malley canvassed many stores and finally tracked down the gun shop Grace-Ellen bought the bullets at.

Grace-Ellen screamed and ranted and raved that it wasn't her, but the guy that sold her the bullets. It seemed like a she said he said moment yet again; until the Bruno's wife stepped up and said that she had seen that woman Grace-Ellen in their shop.

Grace-Ellen decided to give them the lowdown; at least her version of the truth. She still continued to claim she was a battered wife and she had enough she took my gun for protection and bought the bullets only to protect herself. She almost had them believing it but the first guy she tried to hire to knock off her husband came forward and put the kibosh on that. She'd promised him herself and a lot of money but he was playing for the other team and he wasn't interested. Grace-Ellen ranted and raved about that one and threatened to reveal his sexuality. She kept calling the man a poof.

He told them her that he didn't care what she said, he didn't liked the opposite sex and people would just have to accept him. He then confessed that Grace-Ellen had been plotting all this for a while and I was just the patsy she picked. Seemed like nice enough fellow. Maybe people should live and live. What happens behind closed doors aint no business of mine or yours, I'm thinking. Of course the man had just saved my hiney and I was grateful.

When Pat started searching the system from state to state a minor miracle occurred Pat reached the right ears and eyes.

Mrs. Grace-Ellen Parks had done this before in three
different states, each time picking out a patsy for the fall
guy. She was a black widow, getting rich of the proceeds of
each of her husbands' demise. One of those men she had
conned had been hung for her crime; the other two awaited
their execution in the electric chair. The cops who had
convicted the men drove to our town and when they saw
Grace-Ellen they were able to identify her under several
different names. Turns out the one flatfoot said Grace-Ellen
wasn't even her real name. Her name was really Eunice
Perkins from Arley Alabama. Seems they wanted her there
too. She'd killed her whole family there and took every
penny they had. As for me, I'm very grateful to Pat
O'Malley for saving my bacon.

Pat is a gem. She loves being a cop; despite the fact that
they don't respect her. She is better than most those cops at
her precinct but they stick her with typing jobs and traffic
patrol. All those jobs that none of them want to do. Pat
wasn't just a police administrator I could banter with; she
was a woman and a darn good investigator. She was the one
that tracked down all the information on that woman. Damn
those other flatfeet. I hated that they didn't respect her. I
wore Pat down and we started seeing each other quite a bit.
What can I say I'm a sucker for tears and when she cried
because I was free, I saw Pat in a new light. She didn't even
throw my fumble in my face and when I glanced at her, I
saw true beauty and grit.

Pat and I began a dance. I'd soirée her around from time to
time and sometimes she'd pretend that is what she wanted.
Other times she would date a fellow cop. A mistake of I
ever saw one but you can't tell someone you're the guy for
them. I'd wear her down, I vowed.

Summer turned into autumn and I took her to the Harvest dance. We danced the night away and I was convinced I had her in the palm of my hand when he walked in...Sergeant Ray Walters. He told Pat he'd been looking forward to meeting one of his fellow flatfeet. Who pointed Patty out I don't know; but they didn't do either of us any favors.

. I hated him from the minute I met him. Most of all I hated the way he brought a smile to Pat. She was my Patty not his except she wasn't. She thought Ray After that every word out of Patty's mouth was Ray did this Ray said this....RAY,RAY,RAY!!!

What a fire extinguisher. How I hated that name. He was a cake-eater, making a play for every woman near him but did Pat see that? She did not! She cast a kitten when I brought it up and accused me of lying and being jealous. Hell yes, I was jealous but I didn't lie.

I was dizzy for the dame, but Sergeant Ray Walters wormed his way into Pat's heart. She forgot all about me. Some say I should have been more forgiving and thought only of her happiness; but I really believed I was he was a crumb bum. I knew he was; the world just didn't know it and was my turn to prove it. Ray might have the bulge, but I had the muscles and Ray would go down if he was who I thought he was and if he was a good guy then he'd have my blessing and I back off. Patsy deserved happiness even if it wasn't with me.

I started investigating the guy. Scouting him wasn't easy. I had to dress up like a sweet patootie. Even my own dearly departed mom wouldn't have recognized me. I was a looker, a hot mama, if those wolf whistles I got walking down the street were anything to go by. I sought my quarry and watched him pretending to be a good time girl hoping he wouldn't run me in. It wouldn't look good on my rap sheet.

I watched like a hawk as he patrolled the street. I saw him rough up a couple of no good torpedoes. a hustle them off to some cells. He gave some jaywalking tickets to some very pissed off citizens. My surveillance was not paying off.

This should have made me back off, but it made me more determined. Ray was dirty I knew it. I watched him for another week; toning down the costume I wore I dressed as an older woman, a bum off the street. I looked hideous with blackened teeth and a smell that would chase a dog away. He'd never recognize me and neither would Patty if I came across her.

I spotted the asshole taking bribes and pulling out my camera. I clicked off a few shots got some he didn't notice but the last one I took where the dame we all knew as the Mayor's wife kissed him and gave him the cash his eyes opened in shock . The flash alerted him though and he ran after me I barely made it into a building where I had hidden my real clothes. There I dispensed with my get-up and hid out until the goombah left. I went to my rooms developed the shots and I then took my pictures to the district attorney and internal affairs. They put the pinch on him. Ha ha!

I had to testify and for awhile Pat was mad at me. My abundant charm however won her over that and the fourteen carat diamond she wore on her finger as a promise that come we'd marry. (I'd had to work day and night for some bigwig to earn the dough for six months but it was worth it)

A short time later and I showed her my wedding present to her. They'll be no more women tricking this P.I. I've got a partner now and the name on the door in gold lettering is Jack and Pat Forbes Private Investigators.

~0~

If you enjoyed this story read on for more of Jack's adventures in the next story

.

Forbes Investigations

F riday morning and the ball and chain wore me out.

She'd called me six times in the last hour. Times had been tough, since we said I do. My detective business had dropped off, since I stopped using the standard lines on the clients. Ads kept the banker at bay. Ads for books about detectives paid the rent. With my bill pulled down and my face covered no one would recognize me. These chiseled looks could be used for more than being the darb to my broad's bottom line. If the boys knew though I'd never live this down. The work had paid some top lettuce, but now the same work dried up. We needed the dough.

All my other half did was bust my chops about this, since the doc told her one of her hen fruit had taken root and she had to stay in bed like a beached whale. She wouldn't even let me get a buzz on, in case the kid came sooner than next month. Doctor's fees don't come cheap and the girlie needed constant attention with this little whippersnapper. Oh that's right you don't know my Patty. Pattycake as I called her, when no one's around. If I dared to call her that in public she'd take off my head.

She becomes jealous of every good looking dame that comes through my office door. Pat used to work with me, but since she's been laid up she keeps imagining the worst. Granted I used to be sap for the hoofers and for the dames that frequented my office, but that was before I met her. She says I'm a fall guy just waiting to happen.

A pushover when it comes to a pretty face and nice pair of gams. What a bum rap! You think a man's spouse would have some faith in him!

She just continues to think I'm in cahoots with every dolly that comes in the door; especially those Dumb Dora's that prance around in the swimsuits, during the ad campaigns. Patricia O'Malley-Forbes keeps insisting I'm on active duty and on the prowl. I told her she was the only gal for me and why didn't she dump her Daddy's name, now that she had mine? She laughed and acted like I was some kind of lounge lizard. So I changed the subject and Patty asked me if she was fat.

No do I look like a fat head? I told her she still had the best gams I'd ever seen. Even that didn't make Patty smile.

I want my Sheba back, the dang kid sucks the life right out of her, like that book I read Dracula. What? Yes I admit it I read so what! It gets pretty boring waiting on some fancy man to come along and pinch some fellow's wife, so you can get it all on camera.

I moved my chair back and forth across the floor in sheer boredom, when I heard a knock at my office door. It was slight but I heard it. Walking across the floor, I threw open the door to someone who gave me the heebie-jeebies. The man was a mountain his shoulder as wide as the door and just as big around. His fist was as big as my head and his feet? I don't know where he found shoes big enough.

"You Forbes? Which one Pat, or Jack?"

"I'm Jack," I answered putting out my hand. He took my hand and squeezed. I thought my hand would break but didn't flinch.

"You'll do boy. I got a job for you."

"I get thirty bills a day." I explained, "What's the job?"

"It's a delicate job. One that must be handled with decorum."

"DE what um? I asked confused.

"Politeness and the utmost secrecy."

"That's my middle name," I replied.

"My guys all say my wife stepped out on me. Jane wouldn't do that. You have to prove that she isn't."

"And if she's do the nasty?"

"Don't be vulgar, my Jane would never..."

"Mr?" I asked.

"Mr. Darcy. You can call Mr. Darcy...that's what my Jane calls me."

"That's what you want me to prove, that she does not step out on you?"

"Yes, now you speak my language...I mean yes, that is correct," Mr. Darcy answered.

"So where can I find the dame?"

"You will speak of Jane with respect," Mr. Darcy admonished.

"Sorry, where can I find Miss Jane?"

"She tells me she's in the choir. You can find her at the church," Mr. Darcy answered.

"Do you have a picture of the saintly Miss Jane?"

"Watch your lip, or you'll be sporting cement shoes and swimming with the fishes! Capish?"

"Yes sir," I exclaimed.

The guy's language had changed on a dime. I was in the presence of a wise guy. Dare I take on this job? Dare I not?"

"Just to show you I'm a fair guy. I'll give you fifty smackers seeing as I heard your wife expects a bambino.

Here's my Jane's picture."

"Thank you," I replied. The money would pay the doctor's bill for delivering my kid, but it made me uneasy knowing he knew about my child.

The man slapped down the money and exclaimed, "I'll be back tomorrow night for the goods."

He then slammed the door of my office on the way out. I sauntered over to the church sneaking in the back way to spy on the moll. She wasn't there lots of others singing but no sign of Jane. What did she hid? Could I find out should I? First I needed to wet my whistle. I looked for the nearest gin mill. Entering through the doors I almost turned around this place was too swanky for me. I sauntered over to the counter and the top hat ignored me.

"Hit me up with some giggle water."

"Giggle water?" asked the top hat.

"Scotch neat," I demanded.

He gave me my drink and I paid him twice what it was worth anywhere else. It was then she walked in. Jane was twice as beautiful as her picture. She was blonde statuesque and had a figure that most women would kill for. She then went into the back room and came back dressed in a low cut blouse and an apron. Stepping out she took drink orders.

"Georgia take that man's order," demanded the top hat Looks like she wasn't stepping on Mr. Darcy; she tried to make some dough for some bubbles. Would Mr. Darcy be happy with this explanation after all she flaunted her charms while hawking drinks and in a name not her own. I debated on what to tell him finally I made a decision.

Mr. Darcy came in the next day looking like the cat had kicked him.

"She wasn't at the church was she? I went there and saw you leave."

"I know where she was," I admitted.

"Where?"

"The Bluenose."

"She was at the Bluenose?"

"Yep, hawking drinks."

"She was one of them floozies?" Mr. Darcy exclaimed.

"Never a floozy, she conducted herself with what was that word you used... decorum."

"But why would she work there I give her all the money she needs," Mr. Darcy cried, "Maybe she tried to earn enough money to buy you something," I lied.

"You had better be telling me the truth or you'll be..."

"I know I'll be swimming with the fishes."

"See you tomorrow, Jackie boy and if you tell me lies I'll drop you," Mr. Darcy stated as he left.

Seems I hit the ball on the head, Jane tried to buy Mr.

Darcy something. A new gun he had his eye on. Luckily he didn't use it on me. Aint romance sweet? Sure did make me appreciate my sugarplum more. Jane and Mr. Darcy got married a month later. I just made it to their wedding after being at the hospital all night, where my beloved daughter was born. The kid held my finger and my heart was stolen. I knew Lucinda or Cindy, as we called her would be twisting the same finger for the rest of her life and I couldn't want anything more. As for Patty, that woman was more beautiful for the curves the kid put in her figure. She was the cat's meow, my Sheba had returned. I wanted her more than I ever had before she was the Madonna and Betty Grable all rolled into one. She was a bearcat, a femme fatale of the first order and she was all mine!

"Say sugar, are you claimed?" I asked.

"I don't know sugar, am I taken?" giggled Patty as she suckled Cindy at her breast.

"Always," I answered smiling and smacking my lips on her kisser.

Life was good. I didn't need my giggle water as long as I had my Patty and my precious short stuff Cindy.

~0~

Thank you for reading my story. Please continue on to the biggest mystery of my life.

Chapter 1 - Puzzled

I tasted copper in my mouth and had the smell of burning flesh in my nostrils. I opened my eyes to bright light and pain so, much pain. Where could I be? Though my eyes couldn't seem focus I knew I wondered if I was in hell, because I wasn't a devout Catholic. Hell I was a lapsed one I hadn't been to church or confessional in years.

Pain had inched into every nook and cranny of my body. My hands tingled and felt burnt and did my toes and head. What had happened? Had I been tortured? My body did feel like it had been beaten. The haloed light around everything seemed to be fading, but I realized with growing fear that I was tied down.

My enemies had succeeded they had me!!!

Even though my eyes would not seem to focus; I tried to move, pulling this way and that but the ties that bound me were too strong. A huge man with a smug look on his face came into focus. He held me down with a paw like a lumbering bear and moved me easily down a long hall with bright lights and into a room on a stretcher. My mind couldn't seem to take in the facts or focus at all, something that wouldn't help my present situation. I needed to clear my mind and then I could accumulate the information I needed, I reasoned. The lumbering giant untied me and placed me in a bed with soft warm sheets and then closed the door and left. I was in a stark white room with no furniture other than a bed and a window which had glass but on the other side was a screen mesh that was impenetrable. Where was I?

"Are you calm now Johnny? Relax it's all over now," a soft melodic voice, of a woman dressed all in a white reassured.

Where had she come from I wondered. I thought I was alone but then this dizzy dame appeared as if by magic. It was all peculiar and frightening. For a minute I thought I'd blown my wig but that was ridiculous. I was as same as the next guy.

The woman in a white coat sat in a chair next to the bed they moved me in to. The white coat was a dame. What a novelty, but why was a doctor attending me? What had happened? I stared at her taking in her stunning beauty. Her chocolate brown hair was held in some kind of ball at the nape of her neck and she wore a long shapely skirt that just touched her calves. Her white blouse touched her neck indulgently, covering up her sensuality but there was no disguising her large breasts. Who was she? And why did she hold me in bonds?

Weak as a kitten and shaking, I tried to get warm pulling the sheet with my now released fingers, up to my neck. She called me Johnny, but no one had called me that for years... not since I'd changed my name from Giovanni Fabbrizzo to Jack Forbes. I had moved out of the neighborhood away from the bad influences that Great Aunt Fanny and ma would have frowned upon. Somehow Jack (my childhood nickname) reassured my clients Giovanni, or Johnny; the name the neighborhood had called me, didn't. So she must be from the neighborhood I grew up in.

The neighborhood I had grown up in south Detroit had been a gangsters dream, small rundown apartments full of poor trodden down families some of them willingly to do anything for a buck. Some of the neighborhood kids myself included had run errands for Tony the Tuna just to bring in a little cash to our dirt poor families. Most of those children didn't have a great-aunt Fanny raising them, who beat their asses with a wooden spoon when they caught them red-handed running errands for the mob. I had been twelve when I participated in that endeavour, something I regretted to this day. Number running was common place and the kids that helped them hide the criminal activities were a familiar sight but not in Great Aunt Fanny's sight. I was already on my way to higher aspects of criminal activities when Great Aunt Fanny saved me.

Great Aunt Fanny had risked life and limb on my behalf entering the den of the lion to get back my soul from Tony the Tuna and get me out of his orb. Tony had a lot of respect for my great-aunt Fanny so when she had begged him not to involve me anymore in his business at first he laughed, but then he agreed. He liked her spunk and the fact that she had brought me with her beating me about the head every time I tried to speak up. He favored me with protection from harm in the neighborhood and some not so favorable contacts with some of his buddies in my private investigator business I started much later. He kept it secret from his bosses that I was alive.

It was Great-aunt Fanny who directed me into the private investigator business. I completed my first case at seventeen years old retrieving a lost bracelet belonging to Great-Aunt Fanny's best friend. Turns out the bracelet hadn't been lost but stolen by her ball and chain and sold to buy baubles for his dolly on the side. Great-Aunt Fanny's best friend had (with my help and a few choice pictures) received a divorce from that lowlife and some cash to compensate her losses.

I had operated as a private investigator for quite awhile now. I had clients who relied on me to find the goods on the people they needed to be in the know of but my greatest funds came from peeping on husbands and wives steppin' out.

Great-Aunt Fanny passed away just after my eighteenth birthday but I had regulars who kept me flush enough to pay the rent of my offices, the fees for my brother's schooling and the rent on my room. Women were a dime a dozen and they seemed to buzz in and out of my life. I'd met no one I cared to keep around. So I was footloose and fancy free, as Great-Aunt Fanny used to say. Could I have slept with the wrong woman and her paramour had come after me? How or why had I been brought to hospital? Why did I feel like someone had been torturing me?

The woman shimmed her chair gathering herself closer to me, and interrupted my thoughts asking, "Do you remember me Johnny?"

I shook my head.

"I'm your doctor. Doctor Capello," she explained.

Frankly her beauty had almost lost its charms for me. Something about her stirred hatred and fear in me. She was a doctor yet she tortured me? Why? What had I done to her? Was she in cahoots with the butter and egg man that hired me? What a minute, who had hired me? I didn't remember the last case I was on. I remembered working on a divorce case where I earned some cabbage taking some shutter on a dame who was steppin' out on her Joe. But that had ended peacefully. The woman had taken up with her sugar daddy and was now the new Mrs. after her divorce; it couldn't be that case. What had gotten me in to this prediction?

"I know that treatment was painful, but if I didn't think this treatment would work we wouldn't put you through this," Doctor Capello continued.

"Where am I?"I croaked.

She put a glass of water to my lips and I sipped deeply and sputtered as I choked on it.

"Drink slowly," she ordered then she answered my question "You're at Shady Rest."

"You think I blew my wig? I assure you I am sane."

"Johnny, do you remember the last six months?"

"Of course I do," I protested even as I knew I did not. "And the name isn't Johnny... the name is Jack...Jack Forbes you've obviously mistaken me for someone else."

I saw her almost shake her head then stop in mid shake. My eyes grew heavy and I felt so tired and my body felt like all the nerve endings had been singed.

"You're tired from your treatment. Sleep well. We'll talk some more later. Don't worry we'll talk about the last six months."

I wanted to talk about it now but it seemed my body didn't agree as I involuntarily closed my eyes falling into a deep sleep.

~0~

Chapter 2 - Patience is its own reward

My eyes took in the image of my office door, black lettering which said Forbes and Forbes. I shook my head, nothing seemed right even in this dream. I traced the letter with a finger and something inside me chilled. My stomach churned and my brain refused to retrieve the first name of the other Forbes. I pushed open the door and suddenly I was in a cabin, not my office. I saw a figure standing over someone deep in the shadows, at the back of the chalet. Torn between wanting to advance or retreat, as my heart pounded in my chest, I made a decision to withdraw. The opaque shape floated across in inky blackness that seemed to envelop everything it touched. It honed on me like I was a beacon, moving with lightning speed through the room. Almost undecipherable, the character came upon me and bony fingers reached for me beckoning me closer. Terror gripped me and I shouted no and begged to wake up.

I woke up my eyes feeling like sand had wormed their way into the back of them. I jumped from my bed and felt my knees try to give up the ghost on me. Good lord, I was barely thirty...okay thirty-five, had I been that ill? I pulled myself upright and went to the door. I turned the knob to find it locked. Someone had locked me in. I had to find a way out.

My greatest asset? Patience! I would escape these people's clutches but first I'd find out why they held me.

I rattled the knob again and felt the handle being jerked out of my hands as the door then opened.

"Good morning, Jack," the man said.

He was tall over six feet and built like a wrestler. His chrome dome shone under the bright lights and his white pants and shirt indicated he was either a male nurse, or an orderly.

"Good morning," I answered cautiously.

"Do you remember me? I'm Barry your personal nurse."

I nodded I didn't really remember him but he seemed almost puppy dog like and I didn't want to disappoint him.

"Ready for your shower? We've got to move fast, meds are in ten minutes and you know how Nurse Hammerston flips out if we're late."

"Nurse Hammer?"

"You've got that right Jack."

He hustled me to the showers. As I showered I checked my body for the reason for my hospitalization. My brain still foggy, told me I had imagined the scenario where I was a prisoner, but I found a second healed bullet wound over where my heart should be. I gave thanks for the genetic mutation that had saved me from my demise.
Having my heart on the right side had saved me again. My twin brother, Giancarlo had perished at birth, but his presence in the womb had made God model me to mirror him. I noticed my ribs sticking out. I'd lost a lot of weight I couldn't afford to lose. My wrists also bore scars I hadn't seen before either.

I slipped on the draw string pajamas and the shirt Barry offered and we travelled down the hall and into a cafeteria like area. Barry pointed to the line and motioned for me to get into it. Nurse Hammerston handed me some pills and I took them swallowing them. I felt slightly buzzed and then I found myself waking up in that bed again.

Where had the day gone and how had I gotten back here? I got up out of the bed and went to the door. God damn it, locked again. I was a prisoner and they'd drugged me. Who held me prisoner, and why? I rattled the door again and Barry answered it.

"Feeling better, Mr. Fabbrizzo?" Barry asked.

I stared at him. But why did he call me Mr. Fabbrizzo today? Why not Jack?

"Yes, fine Barry," I answered.

"It's Garry today, Barry's twin brother remember?" Garry answered.

Why couldn't I remember how I got here? Was it the drugs? I needed a horn to call some trigger men that could bust me out of here. I thought about running past him, but Garry was a mountain and I was all skin and bones weakened from whatever had happened to me. I'd wait until I got back some strength then someone would be in the slammer.

"Group is in a half an hour," Garry announced.

"What the hell is group? I need a shower, and breakfast," I complained.

"You had a phobia to the water yesterday and today you want two showers?"

Two showers? What the hell was this goon talking about?

"I didn't shower today and I'm hungry," I protested loudly.

"Calm down now. You had breakfast this morning and lunch an hour ago. Do you need the wheelchair, or do you feel you can walk today?"

Today? I'd done this before? They wouldn't get the drop on me again. I'd palm those pills next time.

"Hurry up, Doctor Carvello wants to see you after group. You have an authentic visitor coming."

Authentic visitor? Was Garry playing games with me; insinuating that I had made up one before? Who was this mysterious visitor? If I couldn't get some straight answers out of the mysterious Doctor Capello about why I was being drugged and held here, I would get some answers out of this visitor.

Did they think I'd lost it? I had all my marbles and I wouldn't play their games. They thought they were so cunning but I'd be out of here by days end. For now though I'd string them along and go to this group, they spoke of.

Group was a bunch of idiots nattering on about problems and how they couldn't handle them. What kind of fools can't handle what life throws at you? Talking about it doesn't make it better, best to forget and move on. That had always worked for me and I was about to blather now.

Some degenerate guy started raving about the voices in his head and I thought this would be my chance to escape, but it turned out Garry watched me like a hawk. They got that guy settled down and hauled him off to his room. Then I was beckoned forth by Barry to take my pills, as they all lined up.

I began to think I had been inserted in a loony tunes bin and they expected me to crack. While no dice for them. Jack Forbes didn't crack no matter what you threw at him he triumphed. I'd get out of here sooner or later. They'd better watch out I'd make them pay for all their transgressions.

I obedient lined up, but I didn't plan on take those pills. Nurse Hammer pushed the pills into my hands and I pretended to take them slipping them under my tongue. Unfortunately that witch was on to me and got Garry to hold my arms, while she shoved them down my throat. What she didn't know was that I had palmed one of them. What the other ones would do to me I didn't know, but sometimes the greatest victories are the small ones.

Doctor Carvello ushered me into an office and bid me sit down. I obeyed I was curious about these visitors.

"Do you know why you're here Johnny?" she asked.

"The name is Jack. Jack Forbes. Only people who are close to me call me Johnny and you ain't one," I commented.

"Johnny you do know me. Do you know why you're here?"

I found my head shaking of its own accord and she frowned slightly. She then motioned Barry to take me to my visitor but was interrupted by a woman barging into her office.

"Andrea...oh I'm sorry I didn't know you had a patient in here," she cried then seeing my face she added, "Mr. Fabbrizzo, is really you? You're so emaciated," the woman then turned her head to Doctor Carvello and said, "Andrea you need to fatten the man up. He looks terrible." then turning back to me again she continued, "I was sorry to hear about what happened to you, Mr. Fabbrizzo and..."

Doctor Carvello seemed to caution the woman not to say anything more with a shake of her head. Andrea looked like she wanted to say more but she was cut off again by Doctor Carvello insisting, "Angela why aren't you in school? You shouldn't be here and you didn't see Mr. Fabbrizzo,"

"But Andrea you said..."

Doctor Carvello shook her head again and Angela continued, "Fine then. We'll talk later. 'Kay?"

"See you later Angela."

"Sorry about that Johnny, let's go see your visitor."

Why didn't she want anyone to know where I was? Why had she cut Andrea off? It seemed obvious this was Doctor Carvello's younger sister as they looked so much alike. The girl looked to be a teen, perhaps fourteen or fifteen years old. So they both knew me from what the old neighborhood? Were they holding me prisoner, or protecting me? I was so confused and I had to admit to myself it couldn't be only the drugs. What had happened to me? Perhaps the visitor could enlighten me? Or I could make them tell me.

We entered a small room with chairs and a sofa and I sat on it facing the visitor who sat in the chair. He looked familiar but I could not place him at first.

Then it came to me. This was George Abernathy my friend, but somehow he seemed eerily older.

"Jackie, my boy, you're looking so much better after a month here. Sorry, Samuel couldn't come but he'll be here tomorrow."

I'd been here a month and now my brother visited me? Sam wouldn't have stayed away. What had happened to prevent that? Sam wouldn't let me languish here! They'd obviously lied to him. Sam would rescue me in a heartbeat, but maybe he wouldn't need to if I got through to George. I didn't say anything and he continued talking.

"Jackie, I'm sorry. If I'd known they took you to that place..."

"Place, what place," I asked.

The hospital sent you to that Schuler Mental Institute. That shrink should look after his own issues instead of treating patients like he knows what he's doing," George cried angrily.

I looked over at Doctor Carvello and she had put a finger up to her lips to silence him. He didn't see it.

"When you cut your wrists they took you there and I didn't find out for six months but when I did...when I found out what they did to you...Torturing you like that...with that damn zapper."

George looked pained here like he was really upset then he continued, "I should have shocked him after all you've been through. But I contacted the good doctor here and she assured me that she can help you."

"What the hell, do you speak of George? I wouldn't slit my wrists. This is obviously a frame up. Get me out of this hellhole."

"I can't you need this and I need you to stay here and get well, Jack."

"George I'm fine. Please, don't let them keep me captive here. Don't be a part of all these shenanigans. Can't you see they've lied to you?"
George just put his face in his hands and I looked away for a minute and he was gone and I was in a common room with the other patients. Quite frankly, I don't know how I got there maybe it was the drugs that colored my mind and made me forget.

Patients put together jigsaw puzzles and other stared into space. One woman very childlike and tiny rocked herself back and forth singing something unintelligible, in her arms was a doll. Somehow that freaked me out even more. Garry came up to me and said, "Your brother, Sam is here."

"Thanks Garry."

"It's Barry today, Jack. Garry was with you yesterday when you met with Mr. Abernathy."

I looked at the man and realized he told the truth, this was Barry. How in the hell had I lost another day? Why couldn't I tell them apart? Never mind, all would be fine; after I saw Sam he'd get me out of here.

A gaunt man entered the room his shoulders hunched and his head down like he was afraid to look at anyone in the room. When he got closer to me, I looked him full in the face. His hair was dark brown like mine and his eyes, the same color brown and shape as Sam's, but it wasn't Sam. What vile treachery were they playing at? This man was at least five or six years older, than my eighteen year old brother. Did they think the drugs would dull my mind enough to accept him as my brother?

I'd play along for now until I figured out their game. They'd better watch out because I'd escape from here and pay them back for degrading me into thinking I'd lost my marbles and drugging me out of my mind. I stood up to greet my fake brother and was surprised to hear his voice had a timber close to Sam's.

"Jack, you seem so much better. Abernathy was right this doctor is good. Doesn't hurt that she comes from the old neighborhood and is a beauty too, right?"

Doctor Carvello was from our neighborhood? Did she have a grudge against me? I still didn't trust her; but I still questioned what this man was saying he didn't look like Sammy.

"Sam, how long have I been here?" I asked.
"Here? About six months and the other place probably about six months. I'm a terrible brother; after everything you did for me helping me get an education; I should have checked in with you more often. You don't seem to be in the fog now that's good."

"Fog?" I asked.

"The last time you talked to yourself and were convinced I wasn't me."

I had to admit in those few moments, I almost believed that this was Sammy.

"So you became a lawyer?" I uttered the words tumbling out of their own accord. Why did I assume he was a lawyer.

"Yes, I did Jack. I'm glad you remember that much."
He then speaking as I listened, "I thought working hard would get me a partnership in one of those big lawyer firms, but that's not for the likes of us. I need to do what I should have done all along fight for the little people like us and make a difference. I'm fighting for all those patients who've been tortured in Schuler Mental Institute and had to undergo lobotomies and electric shock therapy."

"Electric shock therapy? That's what they did to me isn't it?"

"I heard you were having a few memory gaps. It's expected to happen with the treatment they gave you and the drugs at Schuler. Doctor Carvello says that will get better and you will remember me. You didn't remember me last time. You kept insisting I was not your brother."

"You told me that before. Who are you trying to convince you, or me?" I asked.

"Johnny, please focus I'm not trying to trick you," Sam begged.

So they'd tried to trick me before. It hadn't worked, but they kept trying. Persistent bunch, weren't they?

I continued to listen to him drone on and I had to admit there were times I really believed this was Sammy, but he couldn't have gotten so old unless...

"Jack you can't fool me. I know you doubt me again but I can prove I'm your brother. Ask me something only you and I would know," he insisted.
Torn I asked, "What was my first girlfriend's name?"

"Pick a harder one. Gina DeLaurent, when you were thirteen-years old and I was six."

"Who was the bully that beat you up when you were seven and what did I do to him?"

"Thomas Gallant and you hired Paul Giocoso to whip his ass."

"How did you know that? Who told you someone from the neighborhood?"

"Jack, please think about it," he pleaded.

I'd had enough I just gave him a look that said he wasn't fooling me.
"Fine then, ask me a question only you and I could possibly know."

"What did Great-Aunt Fanny call me when we it was just family?"

"She called me her pumpkin and you her apple dumpling."
He answered, "How else would I know that if I wasn't your
brother?"

I was stunned how could he know that unless...no, how
could six years have passed. Where had they gone? Why
couldn't I remember? If this was Sammy, he thought I
belonged here. Who could save me from this place?

"I'm sorry about what happened to you Jack. It wasn't your
fault. You have to quit blaming yourself."

What did he speak of? What had I done? I put my head in
my hands and heard the woman who rocked in the corner
begin to sing. She sang "Patty cake patty cake, baker's
man." I wanted her to shut-up. I struggled to block out her
sound. Her song then began to crescendo and I wanted to
scream at her to stop, but all I heard were screams in my
head. My hands went over my ears. Then the screams
weren't in my head, but surging from my throat, ear-
splitting and long, as they continued on and on. My arms
flung out and I banged the table. I knew on some level I
was out of control, but it was like I was someone else
looking on as my arms pummeled furniture and it went
flying through the air. I felt arms grab me from behind, a
prick in my arm and then I knew no more.

Chapter 3 - Dreams Turn to Ashes

Dreaming, I saw the floor turn to fog, seeping through and rising everywhere. In shadow, stood a woman in a long trench coat, her long hair shimmering like caramel on a hot fudge sundae. I stepped onto the sidewalk; I strode purposely towards her, but every time I thought I was closer, the figure moved away further.

Finally, I ran towards her in slow motion. Reaching her I touched her shoulder spinning her around; but before I could see her face her body crumbled to dust on the ground in front of me. The figure now a pile of powder; I bent over to touch it. I began scooping up the dust, as if to put the woman back together and felt tears leak from my eyes as I realized the futility of my actions. Then I awoke.

Disoriented and not quite knowing where I was, I found myself trussed to the bed. My arms held fast and my feet trussed too with straps. I wondered what I had done to deserve this and then I remembered. I remembered the uncontrolled anger and the out of body experience and wondered if it was the drugs that had made me act that way. The words of that song what had been the words of that song? Why had it made me scream? I was drawing a blank.

"Oh, good you're awake. Do you feel more like yourself, Jack?" asked Barry.

Ignoring the question I asked, "Can you remove these restraints Barry?"

"Doctor Carvello said those were to remain on until she gave orders that they be removed," Barry insisted.

"I'm sorry about before Barry. I promise that won't happen again."

"I don't know if I should..." Barry continued wavering.

"Come on Barry. I'm not going to hurt anyone, I promise. Please can I have these off?"

"Well, you did recognize me as Barry. That's a good sign. When you're in one of these states you usually don't know who I am."

Puzzled I could believe what he said. This had happened before? What kind of bizarre drugs made a person not remember acting like a crazy fool?

"Okay, Jack, I trust you to behave. Okay? We can't have you trying to escape and throw yourself off the building again."

What in the hell did he speak of? Who told him I tried to jump off a building? Why were people telling such elaborate lies in their plan?

"The doc wants to see you soon, anyway. She told me to bring her to her office if you woke up lucid,"

Barry said removing the straps.

I flexed my hands moved my ankles in a circular motion and wiggled my toes...yep still flexible I'd still be able to escape when the chance came. I bounced upright and swung my legs to the side of the bed; standing on my pins, only to have them collapse underneath me.

"Now Jack, you have to start eating more. You're getting too thin. You look horrible with your bones jutting out and now you need the wheelchair again." scolded Barry, "We're getting some grub first and then I'll take you to see the doc. That will make you less listless and moody. A bit of food makes everyone feel better."

Barry placed me in the wheelchair and I felt foolish. I should be able to walk. What the hell was wrong with me? I'd eat as Barry suggested; maybe it was because I was too thin that I'd lost the strength in my legs. Barry steered me into a kitchen area and up to a table. Barry then placed a bowl of lukewarm oatmeal in front of me. No wonder I'd lost weight were was the steak and potatoes? Or bacon and eggs, this was food for an invalid.

"You're not going to eat it are you?" Barry stated after a few minutes.

I nodded.

"What will you eat then? I'm not supposed to even have you in the kitchen, but I can't bear you looking this way Jack. You're one of my best friends."

Barry was my friend? Then why didn't I recall him? Why did I have big gaps in my memory?

"Jack answer me don't zone out again. What can I make you to eat?"

"I'd like some bacon and eggs, if you could rustle that up," I replied.

"Okay, Jack, but that's heavy food. I hope it doesn't make you sick."

I ate the bacon and eggs savoring each bite the flavors making my stomach feel satisfied as well as my palate. A few seconds later I felt like I would throw up and Barry found a basin. Embarrassed I managed to keep most of it down, but Barry looked guilty.

"You won't tell the doctor what I fed you will you? It's only because Mr. George Abernathy pays sums to the hospital that I got to work here and be your nurse."

"I won't tell! Now, tell me, George hired you?"

"No, I volunteered when I heard about your troubles. I would have worked here for nothing and looked after you if I didn't have to pay the rent. You've been like a brother to me, Jack. You know it was the least I could do for you."

"But your brother Garry works here too."

"Yes, I got my twin brother to work here because you got so confused and excitable when I wasn't here."

"Thanks Barry," I answered and I meant it somehow I knew Barry meant me no harm. I wasn't sure about the others but this big lunk seemed to genuinely look up to me as a friend and I needed one of those.

"We need to go to the Doctor Carvello's office now before she sends out a search party."

Barry then pushed me to her office. My heart began to beat faster, and sweat poured from my armpits. Suddenly frightened to go and visit this doctor and not sure why I uncharacteristically reached out and touched Barry asking, "Will you stay with me, Barry?"

"I'll be right outside when you're done, Jack," soothed Barry.

He pushed me in the room. The walls of her office were yellow, a sickly canary yellow that I hated on sight. I wanted to run or at least hide and this made me more afraid. Why did I feel this way? This was not Jack Forbes. I was a tough private investigator and not some wimp. I pulled myself out of the wheelchair making it to her sofa before sitting down and sitting up tall on it.

"Shall we begin Johnny?" Doctor Carvello asked as Barry left the room and shut the door and I sat on her couch.

My stomach hurt and I wanted to scream no; but I steeled myself and decided to turn the tables on her asking the questions I wanted to know. I sat on the doctor's sofa and started thinking about George Abernathy. When he had visited me in my drug state he had sounded sincere, he was animated and happy, but something about him seemed off. Had something gone wrong in his business?

I needed to get out of here and get back to my life and my friends. I'd fake whatever the doctor wanted to know and then maybe she'd let me go. But first I find out what I needed to know so I could understand what in the blazes had happened to me.

"Are you comfortable Johnny?" Doctor Carvello asked.

I nodded.

There was a knock at the door from the outer office. Doctor Carvello stepped out and I felt the need to spy on her. I crept to the door and listened through the crack of the door.

"I want to see him."

"You can't Sam. You know when he saw you the other day he became violent and then he tried to kill himself. He's not ready to face his past."

"But Andrea, I want to tell him about your engagement. I think it will help."

Offing myself? What nonsense! Why was she lying to keep this so-called Sammy from me? Afraid he'd slip up and make a mistake? I'd never take such a step. She just wanted to bump gums and make him make tracks. I couldn't let her put the kibosh on my getting the lowdown on my stay here.

"He can't handle the stress right now Sam. Keep your voice down and your impassioned pleas to yourself. If he gets a little better we'll discuss it, but I'm sorry you have to go now before he knows you're here."

Go? No way not before I talked to my little brother, he must know something she didn't want him to know. I walked over to the door and said, "I heard what you both said, so you're engaged little brother?"

"I'm not engaged, but Andrea is," Sam admitted.

"She is? Tell me why would I care, whether my doctor was engaged?"

"She's engaged to George Abernathy," Sam declared stepping into the office.

"That's impossible. George is married to Delilah and you are saying Doctor Carvello and he were engaged? He'd never ditch Delilah."

"Delilah died six months ago," Sam insisted.

Delilah was dead? Delilah had been the best woman for George. I had sorted out George's misgivings that Delilah only cared about his money. A little investigating had turned up the fact that she cared about George not his money, although it was a nice perk for her.

Delilah had at first thought a pervert spied on it her when she caught me. She soon got to know me and grew to like me. I'd got to know this beautiful smart, intelligent, giving woman and was even pleased to call her my friend. I'd even been the best man at their wedding. They had a baby...poor little George Junior, his mom dead. How could she be gone? How had George moved on so quickly? I could hardly take this all in. My head ached from thinking about it.

"Is Georgie, okay?" I asked finally.

"He started kindergarten last week," Sam answered.

"Georgie isn't old enough for kindergarten he's only a baby. Why do you lie?"

"Jack, believe me, time has passed. Georgie is five years old."

Sam reached out to me with his hand, but I pulled away this still didn't seem like my younger brother. He'd know not to comfort me. I stared at Sam again. Wrinkles were starting to form at the corners of his mouth and he had more facial hair then I remembered him being able to grow. Time had passed. If this was my brother, I had to trust what he said. Didn't I?

Her, the Doctor *'butter would melt in my mouth'*
Carvello...*her,* I didn't trust!! George had been a widower
six months and he thought of marrying again? She'd tricked
him somehow. She'd been bumping her gums about
inconsequential stuff, while meanwhile she'd been spinning
George round and round while working on his loyalties by
taking care of his sick friend, me and making him dizzy for
her.

The room began to spin in circles like when I got my
migraines. I didn't like any of these turn of events. Sammy
didn't seem like Sam and George thought of marrying this
so called doctor?
I accepted that the man who came to me was George, so
why couldn't I accept this was my brother? I looked at him
again he looked like an older Sammy. Doctor Carvello
looked at me with her fake concern and it made me angry.

"I don't understand the attraction. No offence doc, you're a
hot mama...but this seems awful soon. What did you do to
George to get him to propose so soon? Did you use the
oldest trick in the book, a bun in the oven?"

"Jack...,"Sam rebuked.

"No, Sam, don't push. Johnny needs to process this new
information. He deflects because he tries to understand. Did
you notice he didn't ask how Delilah died?"

"And you don't have to explain me to my brother, unless
this isn't my brother. Now tell me, how did Delilah die? "

"Jack, not this again."

"I think you better go now Sammy. Johnny and I need to talk."

"Maybe my brother should stay," I commented reluctantly to let Sam, if this was Sammy leave.

"Fine, I don't like this, but I'll see you later, Jack."

"Don't let the dame chase you away Sammy."

"I'm just listening to your doctor to make you better Johnny."

Fine, listen to the dizzy dame then! I thought but what I said nonchalantly was, "If you are Sammy, come back soon." They weren't about to evoke emotions from me that would betray my position.

The man who called himself Sam left and she remained. This was a bad business, this cheesy doll, Doctor Carvello had manipulated people I cared about Sam had stood before me. I couldn't keep deny it.

Doctor Carvello even had Sammy twisted around her little finger. Doctor Andrea Carvello pushed my little brother away from me, again. I needed Sammy on my side to get out of here. It was time to play the game, stay calm, put on the charm and get some answers out of her. I hoped my compliance would make her allow Sammy to come back. I would then convince Sammy to take my side. Sammy would then get me the hell out of here and away from her!

I looked at Doctor Carvello and for a moment she seemed very familiar, like I'd met her before, but where had I met Doctor Carvello? Obviously somewhere in my childhood neighborhood, that's what Sammy had said, but where? I tried but the memory was lost...at least for now. I moved on and begged the doctor, "Tell me how Delilah died!"

"I'm going to try to help you remember the gaps in your memory, not fill them in with words," Doctor Carvello stated.

This wasn't going my way, but two could play at her game; I'd just follow my original plan and agree with her. No matter how much it scared me I needed to remember.

"How?" I asked suspiciously.

"Hypnotism."

"Like a magician? Go try your worse. I'm not susceptible," I answered.

"Lie down on my sofa."

I complied stretching out my long legs. I felt silly. She couldn't hypnotize me, only weak people could be put under. Doctor Carvello pulled out a pocket watch on a long chain and told me to watch it as it spun.

"You're eyes get heavy," she said.

I tried to resist, feeling silly, but my eyes suddenly had an oddly heavy feeling.

"You will close your eyes and slip into a deep sleep. But you will still hear me, Johnny, and answer all my questions," Doctor Carvello commanded.

I closed my eyes and fell asleep. When I awoke tears streamed down my face and I felt something awful had occurred. I sat up and wiped my cheeks.

What had Doctor Carvello done to me? Why did I cry? Had it simply been a carnival trick? Much like the magician I'd seen who made others cluck like chickens in his act? I decided it must be, but what had she done to make me cry in front of her?

Emotions threatened to engulf me and I wanted to flee from this room. I pulled up my head as if to sit up then pulled back closing my eyes to regain my composure. Faking an inner calm I didn't feel I then opened them again.

"Johnny, what do you recall?" Doctor Carvello asked bluntly.

"I recalled nothing," I lied.

"Johnny, you need to open up to heal. I know you remember something."

"I don't, now leave me alone," I cried and then regretted giving her and edge.

"Johnny, you'll feel better if you talk," Doctor Carvello insisted.

"When I remember anything, I promise you'll be the first to know. Can I go back to my room now?"

"I rather you went to the dayroom. It's not good to brood Johnny. When you're ready to talk just ask them to ring me," Doctor Carvello replied.

Barry helped me into the wheelchair and took me to the dayroom. I decided to make Doctor Carvello happy and play chess with another resident. The truth was I could have blown my wig. This place was worse than a clip joint. Memories were flowing back to me like someone had slipped me a truth drug. I remembered running out of a building and into the street. Something I didn't quite remember though remained in shadow. Something or someone I definitely needed to know behind a curtain in my mind that would pull back. Every time I tried to focus on it, it slipped away. I concentrated as hard as I could, even though fear made my heart patter, as if it would fly out of my chest.

I closed my eyes and my mind glided me along if I had wings back to that curb and to a woman lying there. It was like I was in two places at once. Seeing and being in that moment at the same time.

The woman who lay there prone and unmoving had long hair that shimmered, like caramel on a hot fudge sundae, but in the tendrils at the ends of her hair matted blood that flowed from a gaping chest wound filled it. With one hand I put my shirt to her wound the other check her neck for a pulse and found none. I looked around for someone else that should have been with her and then clasped her to my breast with the cry of an angry beast.

My head rose up at the start of a car engine. Anger grew and festered within me a lightning red hot rage come over me and when I saw the driver at the wheel their face even though their gender was obscured, I knew I had to stop them. I threw myself into the path of the car, but they didn't stop.

My body broken from my confrontation with the car, I still managed to get up and fire my gun at the wheels of the car. The driver shot back and his bullet hit me in the chest. I fired a shot back and seconds later the car exploded. All of this now ran through my head like a picture reel at a movie theatre.

I opened my eyes and the memory started to fade away but I grabbed it with all of my energy and will and hung on to it like it was a sawbuck. I could have used some dough right now to pay Barry or even Garry to tell me the truth about what happened.

I wanted to know who the woman was who lay dead at the curb and what she meant to me. But who could I ask? Garry wouldn't tell me. Frankly, I trusted no one here, especially not that two-faced Doctor Carvello. Then I realized I did trust someone I trusted Barry. I'd ask him the questions that plagued me the next time I saw him.

He said he was my friend and in that I trusted. The warmth of the sun in the dayroom had me closing my eyes and I fell asleep in the wheelchair.

~0~

Chapter 4 - Patience is a virtue I'm sadly lacking

I awoke my head fuzzy and my mouth full of cotton. Had I been eating the pillow? I heard the jingle of the key in the door and then Barry walked in. Barry searched my face then said, "Good morning, Jack. How do you fare this morning?"

"I'm doing better Barry, after yesterday's session with the doc. I feel less buzzed this morning as well."

"It wasn't yesterday Jack," Barry said quietly.

"It wasn't yesterday? Then when was it?"

"Let's just say awhile ago and leave it at that."

"No, tell me," I demanded.

Barry looked pensive and then responded, "A week ago Jack."

"But how could that be?"

"The doc said it was those meds she gave you. A new drug interacted with the old ones. It nearly killed you Jack. I almost got fired yelling at her. They made me leave for a couple of days," Barry admitted.

"You yelled at Doctor Carvello, for me?"

"Jack you saved my life. Of course, I stood up for you."

"How did I save your life?"

"You don't remember?" Barry asked searching my face then continued, "Of course you don't sorry Jack. I worked at a nursing home that had some unexplained deaths and when they found out someone killed them they fingered me. They had blinkers on. I would have gone to the chair if it weren't for you. You investigated and found out that this woman Andrea Belington had killed them. She considered herself an angel of mercy. She got the chair instead. That's why when I heard about what happened to you, even though I had no psychiatric nurse training I volunteered. Garry on the other hand has always worked in psychiatrics."

"Thanks for telling me, Barry. It's helped clear my fuzzy brain. I vaguely remember that." I lied, "Maybe if you continued telling me of what happened I could remember better."

"I don't know the doc said that would harm your psyche."

"My what?"

"Your spirit would be my guess."

"The doctor doesn't know everything. Look how she messed up my medicines. Please, Barry, I'll tell you what I remember and you can fill in the blanks."
"Okay, I hope I don't regret this, and I'm going to stop if I think you're upset. Cause I'm not very adept at fixing your spirit. So far I've failed," Barry declared.

"Thank you, Barry. You're a real pal."

"So, tell me what you remember."

"I remembered running out of a building and into the street. A woman lay at the curb, a viscous, bloodied mess, and I was so afraid for her."

"You remember Patty?" Barry asked hopefully.

"Of course I do," I lied.

"Describe her then, so I'll believe you," Barry demanded, his eyes narrowing like he didn't believe me.

"Her hair was like caramel on a hot fudge sundae and her hazel eyes twinkled like diamonds, when she laughed," I answered a memory coming back to me.

"Yes, that was Patty. She was a doll. She treated me with respect."

"She laughed a lot. I loved her!" I commented, surprised and feeling an overwhelming loss.

"You did, and she loved you," Barry answered.

"She died," I cried, tears appearing without my conscious knowledge.

I wiped away the tears and felt the horror of the moments when I knew Patty was dead. She had been shot. She was the woman I cradled at the curb. I knew that with every fiber of my being. But why, and by who? The person in the car? Then why did the car blowing up fill me with such horror and dread?

"I think we should stop now Jack. Your wife, Patty wouldn't want you to suffer. She loved you."

Patty was my wife? I'd been married...me, the consummate bachelor? She had to have been one hell of a dame, but then what I remembered of her beauty, if that was only part of the package she must have been the one. It felt right that was my main squeeze...my ball and chain. I felt the pain rip through me to the fiber of my being. I choked back the tears and I pondered the questions that nagged me. Why couldn't I remember her or anything before finding her bloodied by the curb? Her presence lingered on the edges of my mind and I felt her great loss. I wiped away more tears that threatened. I couldn't show Barry how much this affected me, how emasculated I felt by revealing this all-encompassing pain. I had to pull myself together.

Who shot her and why? I couldn't even use her name in my thoughts. What did that mean? I noticed Barry hadn't seemed to notice my distraction and still nattered on so I started listening. I needed answers that my memory just wouldn't give me.

"When you remember some more I'll be glad to fill in some of the blanks but I won't be responsible for sending you back to that state," Barry insisted.

"What state?"

"Suicidal. I couldn't cope if I made you kill yourself."

"I promise. I won't do that Barry."

"You've promised before but you've tried six times."

"What? You're lying! I wouldn't! Only a fool can't handle what life throws at you."

"Or a broken person. No matter what Jack, just remember there are people who care about you. You have good friends and your brother, so don't snow me that you aren't thinking about it."

"I'm not. If I did try suicide before it must have been something I don't remember that caused it. I have to face my demons Barry. I have to remember."

"Give it some time Jack. Even these memories have made you sad and distant. I won't endanger you. Now it's time for your shower and hopefully something edible. We can speak of this later when you've remembered more, until then small talk and recreational therapy in the day room after breakfast."

"I don't like this but I'll drop it for now Barry. Tomorrow will talk of this again," I insisted.

Barry just nodded his head and then steered me to the showers. Another day in the nuthouse for me but if Barry told the truth maybe I did deserve to be here? No, I thought there had to be more to this story. This didn't feel right, but I'd be patient and then I'd get the answers I needed.

What do they say about tomorrow? Tomorrow never comes and yet here I tried to pull more details out of Barry. Barry reneged though and seemed more reluctant to tell me anything of my past. He insisted we'll talk later as he encouraged me to eat and then go visit the ghoul. Okay, so she wasn't a phantom, just a flesh and blood woman who had somehow tricked my best friend into becoming engaged to him. It left an acrid taste in my mouth. Could I really trust her? Trust anyone, let alone Barry? Then I realized this wasn't Barry, but Garry.

"Finally figured it out, eh, Johnny? I'm not my brother, the meek, Barry. You can't twist me around your finger and get me to do your bidding. I won't tell you a damn thing, you ingrate. My brother has been worry himself sick about you and your needs, but not me. If you want to off yourself then do it and quit threatening. Do it now! Go jump off the roof," Garry shouted dramatically.

"That will be enough Garry." Doctor Carvello stated coming into the cafeteria, "You were told to bring the patient to my exam rooms. Why do you berate my patient? Even your recommendation from my fiancé won't protect you from my wrath if you continue to act this way. I suggest you follow through with your duties unless you want to lose your job and any hope of another one."

Hadn't she heard him tell me to kill myself? Even if the
doctor pronouncement made me shiver as if ice dripped
from her words; I couldn't understand why she wasn't
calling him out on telling me to off myself. Nurses stared at
each other like they thought their job on the chopping
block. But Doctor Carvello just stood there like she
appeared frozen in time, pointing towards her office. Then a
woman appeared on the edge of my peripheral view. The
whole room quieted and stilled in her presence. Her caramel
colored hair, framed her heart-shaped face. She smiled at
me and my heart turned over in joy. Then she kissed me full
on the lips. Removing her lips she slapped me on either side
of my face. I didn't understand they said Patty died, but her
she appeared and chastised me like she always had with a
slap.

"Jack, you're imagining all this. Someone is out to harm
you. You have to get your act together buddy. I'm not there
to do this for you. You know this is all an illusion. You
have to get clean of the drugs and remember me and find
out what happened before something bad happens. Only
you can prevent this. So no more feeling sorry for yourself.
Be the Jack I loved!!"

I blinked and she disappeared. I was in the day room, Garry
nearby, but practically ignoring me.

Damn drugs! I'd hallucinated the scene. But real or not,
Patty had warned me of danger and I believed in Patty's
vision. Barry had told me I'd tried to kill myself six times
and I knew I'd never do that.

Could it be the drugs that prompt that and my amnesia? Should I trust the doctor? I went back and forth so many times my head spun.

Doctor Carvello had prescribed the treatment that caused me to fantasize. How much was real? No, I had my facilities didn't I? I'd trust the doctor only so far. From now on I'd protect myself, find the past and get the hell out of here. A small inner voice doubted this though. The voice asked if hallucinations and voices meant I really belonged here? Maybe I should quarantine myself?

No! Doubts would sink me. I'd follow through I'd take no more medicines and palm them when they forced them on me. I'd get clean of them and then maybe things would seem better. I looked over at Garry sideways. I might have hallucinated, but maybe my subconscious through Patty tried to tell me something? I didn't trust Garry? I shouldn't trust Garry? Could I trust Barry? Anyone?

Garry glanced at me and frowned as if sensing what I thought then looked over as we saw Doctor Carvello walking across the room.

"Garry you were to bring Johnny, to my office a half an hour ago," she complained.

"The guy's been tripping and muttering to himself. I waited for him to be lucid, but I'll bring him now Doctor Carvello," Garry replied, sounding oddly subserviently.

Great! Another session with the doctor. Did I want to
remember...did I not? It seems I would have little choice, as
Garry pushed me in a wheelchair, towards her office.
Sitting on her sofa oddly enough I fell asleep.

~0~

Chapter 5 - Hypnotism

I awoke to Doctor Carvello touching my hand. She seemed oddly familiar, like I'd know her before, but I couldn't quite place her. I sat up and she commented, "I think we should try hypnotism again."

"Again?"

"Yes, again don't you remember trying this before?"

"Of course I do," I lied. Do your worst, Doctor Carvello."

"I watched the watch chain pendant go back and forth. As before, my eyes closed involuntary and I began to see some of my past unfold before me.

I remembered I had spent all night on a case. Ethel Hathaway had hired me to find out if her husband sought gambling, wine and song or just other women. If it turned out to be women then she wanted pictures to prove it. She didn't mind the gambling or the drinking, and would generously give him an allowance for those things. Another woman however would not be something she'd turn a blind-eye to.

I lugged my camera and followed him to Big Dan's speakeasy hidden behind the all night diner. Big Dan, an old friend from the neighborhood, let me in despite the fact they were over capacity. I hid my interest in Harold Hathaway by downing several shots of whiskey. Harold Hathaway played all night at blackjack losing continuously and downing drinks as he lost, then tootled off with Suzy Luiz, a hostess at the club. I climbed up a tree and got them in flagrante delicto. I hurried to my office developed the pictures in my darkroom and delivered the bad news to the soon to be divorcee.

She rewarded me with screams shouts, tears, a trip to her bedroom to quote 'screw him over' and finally a check for two thousand big ones for my troubles.

Slightly inebriated from my adventure, I smiled and took in my surroundings as I walked down the street towards my rooming house. Across the street and a short distance up, I spotted a woman walking down the street. Her caboose attracted me first, as it wiggled from side to side, in the tight calf length skirt she wore. A pair of black stockings with the line reaching down to a pair of black pumps below that drew my eyes. Above the skirt I saw a white long sleeve shirt from the back. I longed to see the view I would see of her front, as I was also a breast man.

She carried a blue jacket, obviously warm in the heat of the day. Her caramel colored hair was in a bun at the back of her head. Stepping down the curb to cross the street, I suddenly saw a man approached her from behind grabbing her arm. She looked surprised as her face turned. I ran across the street dodging cars to come to her rescue. Before I even reached her side, she had the man on the ground, one arm twisted behind him and a knee in his back.

This woman was tough and someone to be reckoned with.

Taking in the view I noted her blouse had popped right at peekaboo breast level and was rewarded with a peek of flesh. She hid a large pair of breasts under the shirt normally buttoned to her neck. My kind of woman, indeed!

"Are you alright, Miss," I asked.

"Quite, and that's Officer O'Malley, to you."

It was then I noticed the skirt was a police issued uniform and that her blouse had a badge that read OFFICER PAT O'MALLEY.

"Sorry, Officer O'Malley, sir, er miss," I said awkwardly.

"Thank-you for your help, Mr...?"

"Forbes, Jack Forbes," I answered.

"Oh, I see that Jack Forbes," she answered unimpressed.

"I see my fame precedes me."

"Jack Forbes private investigator, office on the upper east side." she answered, "That will be all now you can go, Mr. Forbes."

She then took out some cuffs out of a belt at her waist and cuffed the man who had dared to touch her and made a move to march him down the street.

"Aw you might want to button your blouse," I cautioned.

"I beg your pardon?" she said. Then looking down she blushed and buttoned it quickly with one hand.

"Goodbye, Mr. Forbes," she stated walking away with her prisoner.

She was a cop and didn't appear to be interested in me, which of course made her all the more attractive. Her morality attracted me most of all.

She was smart, tough and true to the core of her beliefs. It took a few more 'chance' meetings on my part, but I got her to date me. She played it cool about any feelings for me, until a client who tried to take me down brought out her protective instincts.

She saved me from the black widow who had killed her husband and framed me for it. Shortly after she freed me, we married. My Patty, or Patty-cake as I called her, left the police force and joined the firm of Forbes and Forbes. She protected me from the unsavory women she said preyed on my naiveté and was a great addition to all parts of my life. For the first time in my life I was truly happy. Then she became pregnant. Jealous of the life growing in her, that took her away from me, I grew sullen and took on too many cases, but when my daughter Lucinda, or Cindy as we called her was born I was overjoyed.

I felt that this was the true reason for my life to protect and honor this tiny little bundle of life.

Cindy was a bundle of energy from sun up to sundown, but she seemed to save her greatest joy for me. I was her hero. She smiled for me hugged me at every opportunity. Patty and Cindy were the lights of my life. I tried in the dreamlike state to find out what happened the morning I had found Patty dead in the street, but my mind refused to go there. Instead I awoke with tears streaming down my face, howling loudly on the doctor's sofa while Doctor Carvello attempted to comfort me.

An all-encompassing loss took over my body making my chest burn and heart feel like it had ceased to beat. My head ached and I felt like a part of me was dead. I allowed myself a few minutes of sobbing and then I wiped my tears. My beloved Patty was gone, but I had a child to protect. I had to pull myself together and go to my little girl, Cindy.

"Where is she? Where is Cindy," I asked.

I kept repeating the question, but that damn ghoulish doctor refused to answer. At least I believed I had said it aloud, but the truth was I'd asked the question in a whisper. I began to fear the answer wasn't one I wanted to hear, but then I recalled how little I'd seen Sam. Of course, Sammy must be looking after my child. That is where Cindy was. They were protecting Cindy from my breakdown, after her mother's death.

I had to pull myself together for Cindy's sake. I needed to be with my daughter. She must be missing her daddy, bad enough she didn't have a mother how could I have been so self-indulgent to wallow in grief and forget about my daughter?

I pictured her little three year old face, her curly hair the same hue as her mother's. She bounced on our bed first thing in the morning before the sun arose chattering a mile a minute. A bundle of energy, when I looked into her eyes so like my own I saw the best part of me reflected. I saw a future where my daughter could take on the world and go further than any other woman before her. Maybe she could even be president, but not if she didn't have her family by her side. She needed her daddy, now her mama had passed. I needed to be the man Patty had loved and man-up so I could help my daughter. I vowed then and there that I would soon be with my daughter.

"Do you feel better now, Johnny?" asked Doctor Carvello.

I realized I hadn't said anything for awhile and I just nodded.

"Do you remember everything Johnny?" asked Doctor Carvello.

"I remember Patty and or first meeting and most of our life, but I don't remember that day, or why I found her dead at the curb," I answered truthfully then wondered if she had hypnotized me to tell her everything, as I hadn't meant to share that.

"It will come back Johnny. When it does, remember you don't have to deal with this all on your own.

I'm here to help you," she insisted.

I still didn't fully trust her and decided that if my memory did come back of that day she wouldn't be the first person I told.

"When can Sammy bring my daughter?" I asked.

Doctor Carvello looked surprised and then a shadow moved over her face before she answered, "When your memory is truly back, we will discuss this, Johnny." she answered.

"Garry," she motioned through her office door.

"Take Mr. Fabbrizzo to his room and tuck him into his bed. His had a very long difficult session."

Garry came running obediently, pushing that wheelchair I despised and I vowed to get stronger, so I didn't use it anymore. I needed to be strong if not for myself then for my daughter. I needed to see my daughter now. But maybe Doctor Carvello was correct, without my memory and my health; I'd only scare Cindy. I would never want to do to my daughter. So I'd bide my time and then I'd see my little girl and be the daddy she deserved.

Garry then pushed me to my room and tucked me into bed like a small child, where despite my previously racing mind my eyes grew heavy and I fell into a deep sleep.

Chapter 6 - Ten Years?

I awoke feeling oddly different, refreshed and more like myself. I all but leapt out of bed and stood on the floor. No more wheelchair for this guy, but how had I got muscle tone and flesh back over night?

Obviously more time had passed but how much?

Why did I keep losing time?

"Looking good this morning, boss," Barry commented.

"Boss?"

"Did you forget already that you asked me to call you, boss, Jack?"

"I did?"

"No calisthenics this morning?" Barry asked avoiding my question.

"Calisthenics?"

"The push-ups and jumping jacks you've been doing the last six months to keep you from feeling weak."

I followed through and did some exercise and felt even better. My head felt clearer. But why had I lost time again?

"Barry?" I asked as he took me to the showers, "When can I see my daughter?"
"Not this again. Jack.

"Jack, please, calm yourself. Every time you get worked up about this the doctor changes your medicines and then you go away for awhile."

This had happened before? That damn doctor, Doctor Carvello had doctored me feeding me medicines that had made me lose track of time, again. How much time had I lost? How long had I truly been here?

"If I could bring Cindy back, I would, but she's dead," Barry continued.

I think I let out a groan of protest and then I declared, "Dead? She can't be dead. My daughter's not dead."

My daughter was dead? Nonsense! Did Barry lie to me, or did he truly believe this monstrous falsehood?

Because if it was true, I would know!!!

I had to find out information and Barry was my only source. If only I could speak to Sam I knew he'd give me the truth. Sam wouldn't be fooled he'd know what had happened to my little girl and help me find her because I knew I would feel it to my very bones if she were truly gone. I needed to calm myself. Losing my cool, gave that damn doctor and edge I wouldn't give her again. Doctor Carvello couldn't see me like this, or I'd never get my facilities back. Then something occurred to me, if I'd be here a year or even two then I needed to know.

"Barry, how long have I been here?" I asked.

Barry looked like he didn't want to answer the question but something suddenly changed in his demeanor and he answered, "Do you want the honest answer?"

"Yes," I replied firmly.

"The doctor says the stress you went through losing your wife and daughter, caused the memory lapses.

You don't remember, but you've been here ten years, Jack."

Ten years? He had to be lying I thought. It was absurd. Two, I could have accepted but ten?

Yet when I stared at him, I saw the gray hair which had peppered through his scalp. The wrinkles that had formed near his mouth and under his eyes and I knew he told the truth. I swallowed hard and tried to hide my fear and terror at this revelation. If I'd been here ten years, where had my daughter been?

Was she safe and loved? She'd be thirteen, now a little woman. I needed to get out of her and find her.

I only hoped that Lucinda hadn't forgotten her daddy. That Cindy wouldn't hate me for not rescuing her sooner. Someone had to know where my baby was.

Sam would know. He would never let my child down. Sam must be looking after her. Had she seen her daddy like this? Not remembering who he was, or her? How could I have been so selfish as to wallow in the pain and allow Doctor Carvello to drug me so long?

Why Barry thought she was dead I didn't know, but someone had lied to him. I needed to see Sam, so pretending to be docile and cured; I'd ask to see him. I'd get out of this hellhole the first chance I could escape and find my Cindy.

"Barry, could you get Sam to see me?"

"I don't know if I can," Barry answered non-committally.

"Please, Barry. I need to speak to my brother," I pleaded.

"No, promises Jack, but I'll try," Barry agreed.

Barry then escorted me to the dayroom and I pretended to interact with the other patients, but escaping and seeing Sam were the only things on my mind. The day went quickly and though I asked to see Doctor Carvello many times, it seemed she hadn't come in that day. They said something about a sick child. She had children? They also informed me I'd forgotten her not so new name of Doctor Abernathy. It seems in my foggy period she married George. They had been married for nine years. I reminded Barry he promised to go find Sam for me again, but he just frowned. Did he hope I'd forget?

He then escorted me back to my room tucking me in for the night and locked the door behind him.

I couldn't escape that night, so I decided that the best thing would be to get a good night's sleep and tune out the screaming I heard from other rooms down the hall. Tomorrow would be a new day and a new search for the truth and my daughter. We'd be together soon or my name wasn't Jack Forbes, okay so my original name was Giovanni Fabbrizzo, but I'd long since changed it to Jack. I was Jack Forbes and I would be reunited with my daughter.

Chapter 7 - I Remember

I knew I was dreaming, because it was like I appeared in two places. I watched as a voyeur, as my life unfolding in front of me and yet I was also myself as I relived the day Patty died.

It had started out so wonderfully. Patty had told me she was pregnant and we had tenderly made love before the little pumpkin got up and demanded breakfast. The doorbell rang and Patty went to Cindy as she too cried out. I pulled on some clothes and answered the doorbell to Delilah Abernathy.

Huge tears rolled down Delilah's battered face and she held George by her left hand as I ushered her in.

I looked hard and long at her and saw massive bruises on her face and a black eye with skin puckering up beside it. She held her right arm at an angle I knew meant it was broken. George too showed bruises across his tiny face, but appeared mostly unharmed.

"What happened to you, and Georgie, Delilah?" I asked.

"Happened to me?" Delilah asked, dazed.

I felt useless and didn't know what to do. I looked around for Patty and she appeared with Cindy in tow. Cindy saw George brought him in and offered him the toy cars I bought her and one of her new popguns. George and Cindy took turns shooting at one another, while Delilah came in and sat at our kitchen table.

"Delilah, let me help you," Patty cried.
"Patty...,"Delilah cried big soppy tears.

A few minutes later I heard the whole story as she told Patty. George Abernathy had beaten her. He had become jealous of every man that spoke to Delilah. She'd made excuses for him and said he was under a financial strain, but today had been the last draw for Delilah. George had been out all night with his floozies and then come home to accuse Delilah of sleeping with every Tom, Dick and Harry. He had hit her over and over again and when Georgie had tried to come to her rescue, he'd hit Georgie too. She couldn't get away as George's blows hit her resoundingly over and over again. He hit her right arm, as she put it out to protect Georgie from more blows. He kicked, he hit and with every whack, she'd cried out in pain and fear and still he continued. Somehow she managed to protect Georgie by locking him in the closet. She'd allowed George to take her unwillingly to bed where he had again hurt her and when he fell asleep she escaped with Georgie to me.

My head screamed no, my friend wouldn't do this.

He hadn't turned into a goon, but my heart told me that George had changed. He'd lied about so many things lately. So much so that he had me questioning all of his actions. He professed to love Delilah, but I'd seen his absence in Georgie and Delilah's life. Delilah had spent many an hour or a day at our house lately with George telling her he was out of town on business, while he spent time with his dollies. The gifts he gave those call girls made me angry, for I knew how he begrudged Delilah a new dress, or even household funds to put food on their table. The more I thought about it I began to hate George Abernathy and wished I'd never met him; especially when I saw the compassion and anger Patty held in her eyes.

George could never be my friend again.

"How could you have this man as a friend, Jack? You have to lay charges Delilah. We can protect you. Can't we Jack?"

Patty looked torn.

"He's changed Patty. This isn't the same man I became friends with. I don't understand why he's changed, or why he hurt you and Georgie, Delilah. He professed to love you to honor you. Instead he's treating you like one of his possessions. Has he had any financial problems?"

"Financial problems? Do you hear yourself Jack? He hit hurt his wife and child. He has probably broken Delilah's arm. We have to get Delilah to a doctor and then help her lay charges."

"We'll call my pal Eddie Fresco, the intern in a few minutes. He can fix Delilah up on the q-tee and George will be none the wiser. Then we can get Delilah to safety."

"Safety? We'll help her lay charges won't we Jack?" Patty asked again.

"Not even I can protect her from George. He has money resources and he'll make up lies to protect himself that's what rich people do," I answered.

"Then we need to get her out of the city. You'll find someone to get her out safe. Won't you? You must have some contacts."
"I'm fine, George just needs a couple of day's space," protested Delilah.

"You're not fine and neither is Georgie. He hit your child. How can you think about going back to him?" Patty asked.

"I'm not going back. I'll file for divorce."

"He won't let you do that. He'll come after you both. You need to get away." Patty protested, "He'll ruin your life."

"Okay, I'll run, we'll run," Delilah agreed reluctantly.

"So we need a contact, Jack? I've been out of the loop too long to point you in the right direction," Patty commented.

"Talbot Pennington can get her out safely."

"Talbot? But Talbot is a wastrel and a playboy."

"He may be all of that, but he a good man at heart and he owes me a favor."

"Fine, Jack if you think he can help then make the calls to him and Eddie."

I picked up the phone and called Eddie.

"Eddie can you come and help me out with a medical problem?" I asked on the phone.

Rewarded with Eddie's agreement to come to the house in an hour and half, despite me not giving him any details. I then called Talbot and hit my first road block. Talbot wasn't available. His manservant assured me that Talbot would be home this evening, so I knew I'd have to get Delilah to safety first. Our house would be the first place George would look. I told Delilah to take a room at the Biltmore Hotel downtown under the name Stella Roper. I'd bring Eddie to her when he arrived.

I ushered Delilah and Georgie to the front door. My eyes flashed to the curb where a woman shrouded in darkness stepped out of a cab. I thought for a moment I knew the woman who exited from the cab's name, but the name at that moment escaped me. Flames seemed to emit from the woman as she uttered words I didn't understand.

That same woman's fiery breath turned into a bullet as she aimed at Delilah. I ordered her to stop even as the first shot hit the wall behind Delilah. Her next shot hit a running Delilah who managed to get part way down the street. I yelled for Patty to grab my gun and went to stop the woman and tackle her for the gun.

I heard the echo of her third bullet as it struck and killed Delilah. Georgie terrified ran back in my house for help for his mother. Patty ran out seconds later my gun raised aiming at the woman who shot Delilah. Patty fired and the woman's one arm began to bleed, but she didn't drop the gun and Patty kept running towards me at the curb. The woman turned the gun on me, a bullet striking my chest.

My chest burned and I struggled to remain conscious and save my beloved Patty. I lost consciousness for a moment or two, when I became aware, I now held a dead Patty in my arms and found myself howling to the heavens.

My little girl Cindy ran out of the house with towels to assist with the bleeding, Georgie following as to her bidding. I looked around for the gun woman only to realize she followed Cindy and George.

She touched my hand kissed me tenderly and whispered, "We could have been good together, Johnny. But now at least I'll have your children for my troubles."

She thought both Georgie and Cindy were mine?

I tried to protest and I fought her. She pushed me away as if I were a gnat, opening my wound up more. She stepped into a black Plymouth car placing the children in the back. I needed to stop her from taking the children but how? I found myself searching under Patty's body for my gun and found it. I wouldn't let this crazy woman steal the children.

Raising the gun I aimed as it turned the corner and missed hitting a wall. I struggled to stand, bleeding profusely from my chest but managed to run after the car. I shot after the car again attempting to hit the tire and the car exploded in front of my eyes. I dropped to my knees wanting to die. My Patty was dead and now I'd killed not only my Cindy, but Georgie too. I needed to die there was no doubt. I raised my gun and placed it to my temple, but fate intervened and I lost consciousness, before I could pull the trigger. Then I awoke confused. Was that all real? Were they all dead? They couldn't be!

Georgie was alive Sam had said so. He said Georgie had started kindergarten if that was true, then maybe my daughter had to be alive! How had the children survived the blast? They must have got out before I fired at the car. Did that mean that woman was alive? If so who was that woman in the car and why couldn't I picture her face? How did she know me? Who was she?

George had beaten Delilah and he now had now new wife and his son to himself, if I'd heard correctly. Had George sent that woman after me?

Or was this all a coincidence? I needed answers.

But I couldn't trust anyone close to George. Could I trust Barry, or even my brother Sam? I sure as hell didn't trust Doctor Carvello his wife. She'd probably been drugging me for him. I wouldn't play George's game any longer. I had to get Barry to see that I had regained my mind and get the hell away from these people. I needed to escape today. Then and only then, I could find my daughter Cindy and keep her safe.

~0~

Chapter 8 – Betrayal

At the breakfast table, I formulated my plan. I decided to palm a fork at breakfast. The prongs could be used to pick the locks in this place. I'd pick my room first and then any other door I needed to pick. But it would have to wait until tonight when all was quiet.

I bided my time waiting for Barry, only Barry wasn't on today. Garry worked his shift, and my little bullshit detector went off every time I was near him, now. He was a fathead of the worst kin, a real Abercrombie, bumping his gums and saying nothing. He treated me a man of thirty-five, like I was a geezer. He was hardboiled like his brother, burly and big boned, and therefore an obstacle to my plans. I hope that when he took on his other duties tonight he'd stay out of my hair like enough for me to escape.

Garry wouldn't seem to light for the evening. Every time I'd even think about picking the lock, he appeared. I'd have to flit back to the bed and fake sleeping. After hours of playing possum, I finally picked the lock. The corridor dark and dingy, barely lit, I walked slowly looking for places to hide should I be discovered.

The truth? I didn't know the building. I could recall where the dayroom and Doctor Abernathy's office was, but I had no idea where the door to outside was and that could be a problem. Trying doors might trigger some kind of alarm, if this place was really on the up and up. I continued maneuvering down the hallway and noticed some stairs. I tried the door of course it was locked. I tinkered with it using the fork I purloined hoping I wouldn't be caught. I heard a noise and hid behind a nearby pillar as an orderly I never seen before went by. I watched his large girth waddle by as his keys clinked. I snuck quietly behind him and snatched at the dangling keys which hung from his belt hoping he wouldn't feel it or hear me. My old sleight of hand tricks that I had used to augment my meager earnings when I was eighteen (and still feed and clothe my brother) had come in handy. I had the keys to the place and he wasn't the wiser.

Tiptoeing, I decided to break into Doctor Abernathy's office and get a quick look at my file. I had to see what they'd done to me. Surely they would include where my daughter was as well? I skulked in using my ill-gotten keys and went from the outer office to the inner sanctum of the doc. I noticed a picture hidden behind a potted plant and pulled it out to examine it. A family picture it featured George, Doctor Abernathy and two teenagers. One of the teenagers, a boy I recognized as a teenage Georgie, the other a girl I stared at intently. Good lord, her hair, the color of caramel, so like her mother and yet her eyes so like mine.

She appeared to be about twelve or thirteen, but I recognized her it was my Cindy.

Those two bastards had taken my Cindy and were raising her. Had George been behind my shooting and that of my wife's? Had this all been about taking my daughter? Why? Did the good doctor know Cindy was mine? Did Doctor Abernathy know that George had taken my child? Did she just follow George's orders and keep me drugged to help him? Or was she also a victim? No, she wasn't a victim she drugged me.

I heard a noise and hid behind a chair as a guard entered the office checked it over and then left. No time to investigate my file, I decided to get out of here and go to the cops. I'd tell them that these two had conspired to keep me drugged so they could keep my daughter after George murdered my wife.

The only problem I didn't recall all the details and she was a shrink. They'd never trust my story. I needed Sam's legal help to retrieve my daughter, and then I'd deal with those two snakes in the grass.

Creeping back to the stairwell, I easily opened the door and followed the stairs downward. The hallway emptied out into a hallway, which I followed around to an atrium there with glass windows all around. There, I saw my first glimpse of outside.

Moonlight lit the grass that encircled a long driveway. I looked down at my feet and cursed their bareness. I had no choice. I needed to leave, if it meant cut feet so be it. I opened the front door and an alarm began to blare.

Damn it! Why didn't I try the key? Just because it easily
opened, didn't mean it wasn't armed. I wouldn't last long in
bare feet. I needed to find some footwear. I ran across the
field and felt a cold breeze, like winter's chill settling in my
bones. I half expected someone to appear, but it seemed I'd
made it clear away. I needed to find a home nearby break in
quietly, and hopefully find footwear in my size. But all I
saw were fields and trees.

Where in the heck was I?

I continued my journey heading down a road hoping to
reach somewhere soon. I thought I was in the clear, until a
car pulled up behind me. I hid the keys from the institution
down my underwear, hoping they wouldn't think to look
there. Two goons jumped out and grabbed me before I even
had a chance to run.

"Johnny, hop in now. Where do you think you're going?
It's miles to anywhere and you'll freeze to death," Doctor
Abernathy commanded from the passenger seat, like I had a
choice.

"Come on pal, your feistiness is over," one of the goons
said.

Seconds later sandwiched between the two fatheads.

I noticed who drove my good old paly, George Abernathy.
Some pal! He'd stolen years of my life and my child. Damn
that man! Now he had pinched me, they'd drag me back
and I never see my girl.

Doctor Abernathy seemed to be the type of woman who
would do anything her husband said. I blamed them both
for the last ten years. He'd told her to keep me in some kind
of fog, while he raised my daughter that had to be it.

But why? Because I found out he was a wife beater?

Why hadn't they just bumped me off?

I tried to climb over the goon and get out of the car, but only received an elbow in the gut for my troubles.

"Pull the car over, George," Doctor Abernathy ordered.

George obliged and Doctor Abernathy pulled out a needle from her bag and filled it with a liquid. Then telling the goons to hold me down, she stabbed me with it and said, "I wish you stop being so difficult Johnny. It's extremely tedious retrieving you constantly."

"Don't be so meddlesome Andrea. Johnny won't run again. He knows we care about his wellbeing,"

George crooned.

He cared about my wellbeing? Like hell he did. He just wanted me out of his way.

"Close your eyes, Johnny. Yes, that's it. Go to sleep, Johnny. You'll be home soon," Doctor Abernathy soothed.

"Is he out?" George asked.

"Yes, he'll be out for a few hours," Doctor Abernathy answered.

I wasn't quite under and before I succumbed to the fog of the drugs I heard George say, "I thought I'd fracture from telling all those lines. I told you to bump off the bastard years ago. It's time for him to buy the farm. One shot from one of your cocktails.

We could dump him out here in the boondocks.

How would the authorities know?"

"No dice. They'd know," Doctor Abernathy answered.

"He's still a fathead. Shoot him up and make him forget everything, but that moment he hit your car; then incite him to jump and this time let him."

George insisted," Or do you still have a thing for him, like all those years ago?"

I was done for, would I wake up? And it was her!!!

She was the woman who took Georgie and Cindy, was my last thought before I surrendered to a drug induced sleep.

Chapter 9 – Fair-weather Friends

I woke up tied to the bed in that drab little room again, no closer to my little girl. It was still dark, and I think my captors expected me to sleep longer, for no Garry guarded me. I struggled and somehow managed to free one hand and then the other, releasing the bonds also on my feet. I was free, but for how long before they came back. I opened the panel of the grate and found that though they'd searched my room, they hadn't found the remnants of the fork I'd used the first time to escape. They still had the keys though. Damn!

I had some parts of the fork left (a couple of the prongs). I fiddled with the lock and had the rewarded of a clicking sound and the lock opening.

I went down the darkened hall quietly advancing to the front door again; unfortunately I had to go up a staircase to hide from a guard. I heard the guard again and once again advanced up a flight of stairs.

Opening a door, I hid on that floor only to hear the guard again.

Why wouldn't he just go away?

I advanced up the stairs opening the door and found myself in the roof. Hearing footsteps I tried to hide, but there was nowhere to hide. The guard had me now. The door to the roof opened with a bang. The figure that entered the rooftop wasn't a guard, but George Abernathy.

"Well, that was easy. I've got you right where I want you now. Don't I, Jack?" George cried waving a gun.

"Come on George, we're old friends put down the heater."

"Ah, horse-feathers! You fathead! You were just a drugstore cowboy while I was your butter and egg man."

"You think I was your friend because you were wealthy?"

"Yes, and you weren't loyal buddy. You flitted around from tomato to tomato, but I as much as look at a dame and you tell my sweet patootie, Delilah that I stepped out on her."

"I didn't tell Delilah you were cheating on her. We had a bond. We were pals, pals don't snitch."

"Then who did, Jack? She died by your hand, thinking I didn't care about her."

"Have you flipped your lid? I didn't kill Delilah," I insisted.

"Who has been here for the last ten years, Jack?"

"Why?" I asked, "Why did you have Andrea kill them?"

"I didn't kill anyone."

"Keep telling yourself that Jack, but you know you were responsible for four deaths, one of them your own daughter. How do you live with that Jack?"

"It won't wash George. You had them killed. I don't know how you coerced Andrea, but I know you were behind all of this."

"Me? Don't you try to pass the buck; you killed your wife and daughter after you killed Patty."

"Quit lying George. I saw Andrea's picture of the four of you in her office."

"What in the hell do you speak of Jack? You really have become delusional, paly boy. That picture is of my daughter, Lucinda and Georgie."

"Really? You call her Lucinda and you expect me to believe she isn't my Cindy?"

"My Lucinda is ten years old, yours would have been thirteen."

I faltered then could he be telling the truth had I killed Cindy? But how had Georgie survived? No, she had to be alive. He lied. I couldn't have killed my baby.

"It's time, Jackie boy."

"Time for what?"

"Time to take the big sleep," George announced maneuvering me back towards the roof's edge with his gun.

"Don't blow your wig George. I wouldn't betray you like this. You'll have to plug me to make me jump off this roof."

"That could be arranged, but don't you want to end your misery? It would be mostly painless. After all you're a murderer!"

Murderer echoed in my brain. I almost believed him but his story just didn't wash I'd know my daughter anywhere. His daughter wouldn't have Patty's eyes and my smile. I tried to think of a way to disarm George. Just as I advanced towards him the sound of the roof's door clanged as Andrea (I refused to call her anything but her name, as she didn't deserve the title of Doctor anymore) came into view.

"George we agreed this was unnecessary." Andrea grumbled, "I can handle this."

George turned and in an instance, we battled for the gun. His arm chopped me under my kidney, but I kept fighting trying to get the heater. I got my feet up and kicked him in the face. He grabbed my feet and that's when I went for the gun. We rolled from one side of the tarmac of the roof and still he held that gun. Seconds later, I miraculously managed to grab the gun. I jumped up and held it on them.

"You, Andrea get over here and sit here," I commanded and you George sit there arms behind your back."

Strangely enough the threat of lead poisoning had the two of them obeying me.

"Now tell George how it went down Andrea and don't lie, remember who has the gun," I demanded.

"Oh, Johnny, you really need some more of my therapy. I can help you accept what you did," Andrea began.

"Enough! I've got my little friend here who will make you finally both tell the truth," I stated.

"Johnny...,"Andrea began but I stuck the gun in her face and she began shouting, "He coerced me. You begin George. Tell Jack how you spent the night with me before going home and beating your wife and breaking Georgie's arm."

"Shut-up Andrea, George shouted swinging an arm at her.

"Listen George unless you want a bullet in your arm or leg you won't hit her again. Understand paly?"

George shot daggers at me, tried to get up and I shot a bullet near his leg.

"Whatever you say Jackie old pal," George agreed.

"You start George, with your version of the story and then will put it together with Andrea's version.

Then and only then, will we all know the truth," I stated.

Andrea bounced up and cried, "Johnny, please, I only want to help you. I can help you with this crisis," then she tried to throw her arms around me.

I pushed her away waving the gun at her but her nail scrapped my arm.

"Damn it Andrea that hurt. Sit down again, both of you, and quit stalling," I commanded.

"Where do you want me to begin Jack, maybe where you took my wife?" George griped.

"Oh for Pete's sake, how about starting with that morning. Why did Delilah come to my house looking like she'd been in a fight?"

"She was mad at me. I spent all night at the club.

She accused me of cheating on her one thing led to another and the next thing I know I'm striking her.

She just keeps nattering at me so I socked her a few time. Georgie sees us fighting and tries to stop it and gets in between us blocking a blow. I never meant to harm either of them but especially my boy."

"Of course you didn't George," I said trying to get him to tell me more, but he thought me sarcastic and clammed up.

I prodded him with the gun and asked, "George, how did she come to be at my house?"

"After we made up, I went to sleep. Delilah snuck out taking Georgie to your house. Why did you have to entice my wife Jackie? You had your own beautiful wife. I can't believe you shot both of them. So Patty found out you were seeing my wife on the side, you could have smoothed it over. You didn't have to kill them both."

"What? I had no love or affection for Delilah. I thought of her as my sister. I loved my Patty. Patty meant everything to me."

"Then why in the hell did you shoot her and then kill my Delilah?"

"I didn't kill either of them," I insisted through clenched teeth, "But tell me your version of events George. How did the children survive?"

"The children didn't survive, but Georgie did."

"I have the gun, George do you still insist that the picture I saw is of your own daughter?"

"It's not. Don't believe his lie; she is your Cindy, Johnny," Andrea confessed.

"Shut-up Andrea and quit calling him Johnny, his name is Jack he legally changed it and he prefers it."

"What do you care what I call him you want him dead."

"That was all your idea." George insisted, "If you lied about this, what else did you lie about?"

"So, you're starting to see the truth George? How do you think the children survived?" I demanded.

"Andrea tried to save them from you after you killed my Delilah. Then you tried to kill her and the children. Luckily for them they got out of the car before you blew the car up."

"What? I told you, I didn't kill Delilah. Delilah was my friend and as close to me as a sister, but please continue with this fascinating fabrication."

"Georgie saw me on the street and got Andrea to stop the car. Andrea got out if the passenger seat... I mean driver's seat as Georgie got out as well taking Cindy with him. Cindy followed him and then Andrea got out and ran up the stairs to me. You came around the corner and shot at the car. The car blew up and burst into flames and we all thanked God we were alive. Then I saw the bodies bloodied and shot dead. You did that Jack. You!!!!"

"How many times do have to tell you that's not how it happened?"

"You had a wife and a family but did that stop you from moving in on my ball and chain? No, you had her over, romanced her right in front of yours and then counselled her to leave me and take Georgie, kissing her goodbye," George cried wrenching his hands like he'd like to wring my neck.

"George, I admit it. I did counsel Delilah to leave you. I would have sent her out of the city with Georgie to protect her."

"You were leaving your wife and child for mine?"

"George, get it through your head. I loved my Patty-cake and my little Cindy. They were everything to me. I could never have looked at another woman.

You were abusing Delilah and the boy I had to protect them from the likes of you."

"Who were you to decide that I abused them?

Besides Andrea she saw you kissing Delilah, before you shot her dead on the porch. Do you deny that too?"

"I kissed Delilah on the cheek, because I thought I'd never see my friend again, after she left that afternoon."

"I don't understand this. Andrea?"

"Johnny lives under a delusion that keeps him from admitting his wrong doing to protect himself,"

Andrea spouted.

George rolled his eyes looking at her with disdain and disbelief. I could visibly see him wanting to believe me.

"Okay, so I told a little fib. He still kissed her on the cheek," Andrea admitted.

"Georgie and Cindy said you shot their mother, but I never believed them, Andrea," George admitted starting to believe me, "Not once did I question their story, but what Jack tells me is the truth. Isn't it Andrea? You shot them, didn't you, Andrea?"

"No, I told you the truth George. Johnny shot Delilah when she told Patty about her affair with Johnny," Andrea cried outraged and holding up her hands as if to defend herself.

George then looked at me and then at Andrea seeming puzzled. He appeared torn; he didn't know whether to believe me or Andrea. I decided some more evidence was in order to sway him. If I ever wanted down off this roof, I had to have one of them on my side to escape.

"Think about this George why would I have coveted your ball and chain? Why would I? My wife was a beautiful, talented and strong loving woman. Why would I have strayed?"

"I strayed," George answered.

"You've known me a long time George. Have I ever been anything but loyal? Have I ever betrayed a pal?"

"No, you haven't, but Delilah was murdered."

"Yes, and you know in your heart of hearts, it was Andrea that killed her."

"How do you know Jack had an affair with my wife?"

"I saw him kiss her that morning at your place,"

Andrea improvised.

"That's funny because you told me the morning before and then we spent that night together, so I could get even with her."

"You cheated on Delilah with her?" I asked, but I already knew the answer. Andrea had planned and schemed her way into George's life and mine. It had begun the day before my wife was murdered, when Andrea wormed her way into George's bed.

"Why didn't I question this before? You said Andrea, that you had just finished your residency program as a psychiatrist. You had just arrived back in town after your training in New York. How would you have known about any affair? You came to my office and told me that Delilah and Jack had made a fool of me. That Delilah stepped out on me with my best friend, Jack Forbes. Did you fake that picture you showed me?" George demanded Andrea looked shocked and hurt and shook her head no, but George believed me I could tell and so could she.

"I didn't want to believe her Jack, but she showed me pictures of my wife lunching with you at Chez Marcello's," George explained.

"I lunched with Patty, Cindy, Delilah and little Georgie, two days before our wives were murdered.

I never once lunched with your wife on my own."

"You lying bitch!" George yelled at her.

Andrea tried to hide her face and fake tears but George would have none of it.

"Oh God, I am so sorry Jack. I allowed her to cloud my mine against Delilah and against you. This was all a bum rap. She put you in the frame and almost made me put the drop on you. That damn Sheba, twisting the truth at every turn. I even gave her my heater. Oh no, Andrea used the rod received from me to kill Delilah and Patty. I'm complicit in their murders. Tell me how it really happened and how she shot them Jack. Tell me the real truth, if you remember it all," George demanded, "I already know the fairy tale Andrea told. Then we can get even and give her a Chicago overcoat."

"I'm not killing anyone, George. We'll let the flatfeet handle this. But don't think you're in the clear, paly. You helped her keep me drugged for ten years and conspired to keep my daughter from me.

You were going to fit me with cement overshoes."

"Now Jackie, I didn't kill you in all that time. Did I? Give me another chance. Tell me how she committed the crimes."

I decided to lie and let him think only she'd be punished. I'd probably get by one of them, but not both of them after all.

"You're right George since when did we ever let a dame come between our friendship, I claimed and then began telling him what had happened, "I stood on the steps of our house kissed your wife on the cheek and the shot rang out, first one, then another missing, Delilah. Delilah ran to towards the street thinking she fled the gunwoman. I ran towards Andrea to stop her and went to stop her and tackle her for the gun. Before I could reach her the echo of her third bullet struck and killed Delilah. Georgie terrified ran back in my house for help for his mother. Patty ran out seconds later, the gun raised and Andrea's arm began to bleed, but she didn't drop the gun. Patty kept running towards me at the curb and Andrea fired missing her and striking me in the chest. My chest burned and I struggled to remain conscious and save Patty. I lost consciousness for a moment when I woke up Cindy was there, with towels to assist with the bleeding.

Georgie followed her. I looked around for Andrea only to realize she guided the children. Andrea looked at my wounds and wrote me off. She touched my hand kissed me tenderly and whispered, "We could have been good together, Johnny. But now at least I'll have the children for my troubles."

"She did all of that?" George asked believing me at last.

"Yes." I answered then continued, "I tried to protest and I fought her. She pushed me away as if I were a gnat, opening my wound up more. She stepped into car and placed the children in the back. I found myself searching under Patty's body for my gun and found it. Raising the gun I aimed as it turned the corner and missed hitting a wall. I struggled to stand, bleeding profusely from my chest but managed to run after the car. I shot after the car again attempting to hit the tire and the car exploded in front of my eyes."

"Georgie saw me on the street and got Andrea to stop the car. Georgie got out taking Cindy with him.

He ran to me and told me the story but Andrea interrupted and told me we were all in danger from you. Then you appeared as we were on the steps of the building and blew up the car confirming her story," George explained.

"I wanted to snuff you when I found Delilah's body and I would have; but your buddy the sawbuck, Eddie Fresco appeared. I sent Andrea away with the children before your pal saw them. I pretended I'd just come upon the scene. Eddie attended your wounds called an ambulance. Eddie directed you to a private hospital where they'd ask no questions.

The cops didn't even know you'd been at the scene, thanks to him. You tried to kill yourself in the hospital and the staff unable to cope transferred you to the Schuler Mental Institute without telling Doctor Fresco. They were afraid of the repercussions."

"Then how did the two of you find me?"

"Andrea found you."

"How did you find me Andrea?"

"I checked all the hospitals and when they wouldn't let me take you I used Sam. He could move you being next of kin."

"Why hasn't my brother come back Andrea?"

"I convinced him that he made you worse. That you were better off not seeing him."

"You evil bitch. I should shoot you now, for all you've done," I sniped.

"Why don't you kill me Johnny? You don't, because deep down you have feelings for me. You loved me and only me first, before those she-devils turned your head."

"She-devils?" George asked.

"Don't play innocent George you know that your wife and Patty wouldn't leave Johnny alone. They had to have him. They didn't care who they hurt."

"I hadn't seen you since we were fourteen years old and you moved away, Andrea. I didn't know you anymore. How could you think they were rivals for my affections?"

"Oh, Johnny. Call me Andrea like you used."

"I'm not going to call you Andrea," I answered defiantly.

"Why couldn't you have forgotten her?" Andrea asked

Andrea then moved around George her arm outstretched and I realized she'd poked him with a needle.

"What was in that needle?" I asked.

"The same thing I jabbed you with earlier when you accused me of scrapping you. Only George has a lethal dose. I'll soon be a widow. The drug will make you forget those awful women and then you can concentrate on me."

"I should have known a dolly bird would give me the final kiss off. Damn you Andrea, damn you to hell," George cried and then lapsed in unconsciousness.

"Andrea they'll know you killed George. Please use an antidote," I protested.

"No, you'll take the rap George. They'll believe me when I tell them how you escaped and took him prisoner, and I'll keep you locked up for the rest of your life so you'll never be a danger again. We'll be together that way Johnny. I'll make you forget Patty. With George gone will be in the suds. We can go anywhere in the world."

I began to grow afraid I thought the tiredness I felt had been the linger effects from the earlier drugging, but now I knew she had me yet again for as long as she desired. I would never leave her. I'd be her prisoner for life.

"Andrea, I still have the gun, I could shoot you," I stated.

"Maybe but then you wouldn't know about your daughter."

"What have you done with Cindy?"

"I've done nothing to Cindy I'm speaking of our daughter," Andrea said, as I passed out from whatever she'd injected me with dropping the gun.

Chapter 10 - Free at last

I awoke fearful, that although I seemed awake, I was really dead and this was limbo. But touching my legs and arms and giving them a pinch, I knew I was alive. What the heck had just happened? None of this made sense. Memories flowed through my mind of a younger Andrea. I had thought I loved her. Andrea had been my first sexual experience, and when she disappeared out of my life after three months I had heard rumours that she was pregnant.

My second case was my own. I found out what had happened to her and found out she had given birth to my daughter at seven months. My daughter Angela had died shortly after. I didn't speak to Andrea, but I grieved for my daughter. So Andrea had lied. I had no daughter, but my Cindy.

How had I been rescued from the roof and Andrea, if I was alive? I looked around and saw four white walls and in the corner smiling and sitting in a chair near the bed, was Barry.

"I'm so glad you're awake, Jack and I know two others who will also be happy to see you."

"It's good to see your giggle mug, am I'm still a prisoner?"

"No, this is a regular hospital. Sam had the police bring you here after they arrested Doctor Abernathy."

"They arrested her? How?"

"Sam your brother brought a whole passel of coppers who liberated you from Doctor Abernathy's clutches. They also arrested my brother Garry."

"I'm sorry they arrested your brother, Barry."

"He conspired to kill you Jack, how can you say that?"

"I can have compassion for you."

"Thank you, Jack. I'm sorry I wasn't on to them they fooled me."

"And George?"

"I'm sorry Jack; he's dead."

I didn't know how I felt about this but it wasn't relief.

"When can I get out of her and see Sam and my daughter?"

"The doctor is concerned about the after effects of the drug Doctor Abernathy gave you and all ill treatment of you for the last ten years. He believes you need to stay here awhile longer."

"I've been kept a prisoner for ten long years I want to go home or at least see my daughter," I protested.

"If you're patient I'll see if I can sneak Sam and Cindy into the family visiting room," Barry conceded.

"I can see my daughter?"

"Of course you can. You're not a captive."

I'd finally see my daughter would she be happy to see me? What had they told her? Would she rush into my arms?

"You need a shower pal before you see your daughter," Barry commented.

Barry stuck me in that dread wheelchair again and then helped me into the shower. I then was helped into some clothes so I could look good for my daughter and my brother. I needed to gen up on all the latest things but Barry ignored my pleas for books and magazines, but I'd soon see my daughter so I forgot all of that but my joy.

Barry wheeled me into the family room just after breakfast muttering about how risky this was under his breath and that it could put something in jeopardy. Frankly I didn't understand his strange turn, but I ignored his bizarre behaviour and sat awaiting my daughter and my brother's entrance.

Finally after what seemed like a long time killing time, my brother and daughter walked in. Cindy's caramel hair had grown to her waist I cried tears of joy to see my daughter once again. I managed to get out of my wheelchair and hug her, but instead of joy in her eyes (so like mine) they took on a scared and wary look.

"Jack let her go," cried Sam.

"Sorry, I didn't mean to scare you honey." I commented, "I'm just so glad to see my little girl again."

A strange look passed between them and then Cindy kissed me on the cheek and said, "I'm sorry I'm not her, Great-Uncle Johnny. I am named after her though. I wish I was her, for your sake. I'm sure she still loves you."

Flabbergasted I grasped the arm of my wheelchair and sat down.

More lies? What was their game? Why did Cindy lie to me?

Then I looked hard and long at Sammy and he appeared older, much older. He wore a shirt with short sleeves and an alligator on the breast of it. His pants were casual much too casual for an up and coming lawyer. Sammy's hair had turned pure white and wrinkles were at the corners of his mouth.

He stooped and leaned on a cane.

I didn't understand any of this. Barry had told me that I would meet my brother and daughter.

Hadn't he? They weren't lying to me; I had to admit I'd lied to myself again.

Time had passed again, but how much time and where had I gone? Had the drug that Andrea injected me with done this?

"How old are you Sammy?" I asked.

"I'm seventy-four years old Johnny," Sammy answered.

"Are you okay, Johnny?" Sammy asked, concerned.

"Okay? If you're seventy-four, that would make me eighty-one. I'm not eighty-one," I denied.

"Johnny you are. You are as much as an old geezer as I am," he insisted.

I looked down at my hands and saw wrinkles I'd never noticed before. My whole body looked frail, rumpled and creased. Frankly I looked folded once and dried twice. Sammy told the truth, I was old.

But where was my daughter?

"Johnny I'm sorry...,"Sammy began.

"Sorry for what?"

"Sorry, about not visiting you more over the years.

They told me that you got worse every time I saw you. Your doctor recently saw improvements and thought you would see me, finally!"

"What about my daughter? Why didn't she come?"

Sammy looked over at a man in white coat nearby who nodded at him. Sammy looked unhappy, but resigned.

"Johnny I don't know how to tell you this..."

"Just spit it out," I declared.

"Do you remember the day Delilah died?"

"Yes, Andrea shot her then shot me, then shot my Patty."

"That's correct, but do you remember what happened next?" Sammy asked gently.

"Andrea took Georgie and Cindy and got in a car after shooting me and kissing me goodbye. I shot at the car and the car blew up, but Andrea got the kids out and then took off with George."

"That's not exactly how it happened, Johnny. I like your version better, but you know in your heart it didn't happen that way."

"Grandpa please, don't make him remember. It will only hurt him," Cindy begged.

What did she mean?

"Johnny you have to remember," Sammy insisted.

I closed my eyes and the memory came rushing back. I passed out for seconds from the wound after Andrea took the children in the car. I saw the car ahead and managed to run after it. Imagine my surprise as I saw George in the driver's seat and Andrea beside him in the front seat. Georgie and Andrea looked out the back window at me. I fired at the tire hoping to stop them (but the gas tank had been installed in the back of this model, something I wasn't aware of) and the car exploded in flames.

I remembered I had killed them all. I opened my eyes to Sammy starring in mine.

"You remember it all. Don't you Johnny," Sammy asked.

"Yes," I answered my voice dropping to almost inaudible.

"You remember Andrea shooting you and you trying to stop her and George from taking the children?"

"I did it! I killed them all," I shouted.

"None of this was your fault. Do you understand me? George Abernathy had become obsessed with getting rid of Delilah. When he assumed you had an affair with her, he became enraged telling his mistress Andrea. Yes, the same Andrea who you loved when you were fourteen-years old. Of course, George didn't know that."

"Jack do you feel alright," the man in the white coat asked.

I nodded, but all of this had shaken me and I couldn't quite believe what I remembered. George had tried to kill me? Yet it all rang true, it was actually cathartic in some ways. I could admit my guilt and my remorse to myself.

Sammy continued, "Witnesses close to the scene said Andrea saw your daughter after she shot you and became agitated. She was told to grab Georgie, but she also grabbed Cindy. She stepped into the car at the curb with George at the wheel and you know the rest. You've tried to protect yourself by creating stories over the years where Cindy didn't die, but none of them truly made you forget. Now with this new drug treatment the doctor believes you can face the truth Johnny and so do I. Hear me now Johnny, it wasn't your fault!!"

I escaped all these years with delusion, after delusion, but now I had to face the truth... I killed my little girl and Georgie. All of this had been my fault. Mine!

"Oh, God, please forgive me. Forgive me Patty for not saving you and our daughter; but most of all forgive me for killing our beautiful daughter," I cried tears flowing from my eyes.

I felt heaviness in my chest and my arm felt like a dead weight. Pain raged down my arm and into my fingers, pinging like an electrical wire, firing upon them. I felt my heart speed up, then slow down as I began to sweat profusely.

"He's having a heart attack," I heard the doctor cry from far away, as they laid me on the floor and began ministering to me.

At my side I heard a voice on my left side reciting, *"Jack be nimble. Jack be quick. Jack jump over the candle stick."*

I turned and saw the figure of my three year old daughter Cindy beside me.

"Hello daddy," she cried throwing her arms gently around my shoulders.

"Cindy, is it really you?" I asked.

"Yes, daddy. It's not one of your stories. It's time to forgive yourself. I forgive you and Georgie does too."

"You do?" I asked.

"Course daddy. You taught me that if you do something wrong and you ask forgiveness that makes everything all right, just like Great-Auntie Fanny taught you."

"How do you know about Great-Aunt Fanny? She died before you were born."

"Silly daddy, she's waiting for you. She loves you and mommy too."

"I love you too, baby."

"I know you do and I love you too, daddy, but it's time to go."

"Go? Go where?"

"I tried to tell you Mommy's waiting to see you, but she needs Georgie and me to bring you to her Great-Auntie Fanny, Auntie Delilah, and Uncle Giancarlo.

We're going to have a party," Cindy answered.

"Party? Georgie? I don't understand."

"You are silly daddy. We missed you; so we have a party. Georgie's on your right side."

I looked over to my right and saw five year old Georgie holding out his hand. I took it and stood up.

In my left hand I held Georgie's hand and on my right I held Cindy's hand. We walked down a long foggy hallway. Waiting in the hallway, my Great-Aunt Fanny reached out, smiled and hugged me tight before passing me off to my twin brother Giancarlo. Giancarlo hugged me, smiled and then walked with Great-Aunt Fanny into the bright light further down the long corridor. Delilah smiled at me took Georgie's hand and she too travelled down the hall. I hesitated for a moment and Cindy cried, "Daddy, come on."

Cindy then pulled me down after them and just before I reached a brilliant light, there standing in the doorway was my Patty.

"Hello knucklehead, it took you long enough," Patty said.

"You're not angry with me? Do you forgive me?"

"I'm angry that you wasted your life blaming yourself, but no I could never, ever be angry with you. I love you Jack, there's nothing to forgive."

"I love you too," I answered.

I then hugged her tightly, crying tears of joy, as she hugged me back and Cindy hugged our legs.

"It's time to step into the light with me Jack. Time to let go of your worries and earthly cares."

As I stepped through the door, I heard the doctor say to Sam, "I'm sorry he's gone."

But they were wrong I was at free. Now together with my beloved little girl and my wife I could live out eternity. I had forgiveness at last.

~0~

Thank you for reading these stories. If you have enjoyed these stories, please think about leaving me a few words of review at your favourite retailer and please check out my other books at Amazon ~ amzn.to/1eBlniN

Sincerely S.G.Lee

Excerpt from Stray Bullet

Preface:

In the small town of Driftwood, Colorado, under starry skies, residents went about their business. The town was now ready for the arrival of the new sheriff having gussied up the urban decay with a few coats of paint. The new sheriff would see the bad parts of town soon enough the mayor thought and turned over in his bed and went to sleep. The hospital looking after a few patients was unusually quiet under the full moon; other people in the settlement getting ready for bed and then turning on late night programs or setting alarms and climbing into bed. Across town a man getting ready for bed after a long hard day at work completed his paperwork, stripped naked and stepped into the shower. As the water ran down in torrents the shower glass doors shattered, the man fell to the floor and rivets of blood ran into the drain. He was the first to die that night.

A few doors over gunman entered killing the husband and wife in their beds and the children as they slept. Blood covered the floor and ceilings in those rooms. None of the neighbours heard a peep they simply slumbered on. Other homes across the town were entered and the residents, husband wife and children were also shot and killed. No one had time to shout out or call 911. It was all over in a few minutes with no time for whimpers only the muzzle of silencers doing their jobs and hitman scurrying into the night.

"It's done, boss. The teams are leaving the state. Yes, I'll do that now. He's coming in the morning. I'll check in after I meet him. His name? All I got is G. Bullet not sure of his first name, it's not on any paperwork. . See you, tomorrow… okay Friday," the man said into his prepaid cell phone and then took out sim card breaking it into pieces. Then he discarded it in a nearby bin at the now decrepit old pulp and paper mill. He had to go to work soon. A new sheriff was coming to town and he wanted to be there to greet him.

~0~

Chapter 1 – Friendship Trumps Bullet

My name is G and I'm on my way to a new life to become a sheriff in a town called Driftwood. Sounds boring, doesn't it. If you'd asked me five year ago I would have told you of course it was; but now this is what I need and my daughter needs…a nice quiet life, in a quiet town, where I could raise my daughter without whispers and rumors. You want to more about that statement? I'll get back to that, but I'm told people will want to know about me a subject I'm not really comfortable talking about.

Asked to describe myself I would say I'm tall over six feet…okay six feet five inches. I am muscular as I lift weights. I'm not overly muscular just enough to take down the bad guys. Some people think I look like Tom Selleck in his youth, personally I don't see the resemblance.
G. is a short form for my first name but I don't like to talk about my real first name. Let's just say my parents grew up in the happy-go-lucky seventies and were heavily influenced by the weird names that people gave their children. What you still won't give up? You demand that I tell you my first name? You want to play the guessing game?

My first name is unmentionable I don't talk about it ever!! My last name is wait for it…Bullet…I know a clichéd name if you ever heard one. Honestly, it's my name. It has been mine my whole life.

My last name had raised a few eyebrows can you imagine how many chuckles I've gotten when I tell anyone my full name? Still can't guess? Some of you have deducted correctly. So now you know why I usually don't divulge my first name.

In order for you to understand the relevance of my last name I'll have to explain more about my family and their origins.
My grandfather when escaping persecution in Russia came through at Ellis Island and decided to Anglicizing his name to Bullet; so my dad used that and now I do. What's that you like to know grandpa's original name? Well so would I, unfortunately he took that name to his grave leaving no clues behind. But he was great man, a hard working cop. I come from a long line of cops. With a last name like Bullet it tends to earn respect being a cop.

Grandpa was killed on the job by some backward gangsters bent on destroying one another. My dad swore he never be a cop and went to San Francisco were he promptly fell in love with my mother went to the police academy there and then impregnated my mother.

After I turned one he decided he needed family and got a job as a cop in the city where his father had served and brothers now served as cops. When he worked there for six months he had planned to send for mom and me and marry her. Unfortunately the first day on the job he ran into a domestic situation and was killed in the line of duty. He hadn't told his family about my mother or me so we came as a surprise when mother showed up with me in tow for the funeral.

When I was four years old, my mother learned she was
dying of breast cancer. My dad's three brothers, James,
Bennie, and Alfred also cops, stepped up to raise me. They
were a demanding bunch always pushing me to be strong
and tough. I had to be resilient and learn all the fighting
techniques that they taught. Let's say I am proficient in a
number of fighting techniques.

Their younger sister, my Aunt Louisa was a teacher and just
starting her career when they took me in however Aunt
Louise found time for me. She made my childhood more
normal though my uncles would often say she shouldn't
coddle me. My uncles drove her away with their constant
beratement and by the time I was in my teens she moved to
teach in Colorado to save her sanity. She still managed to
chide the uncles into letting me visit her in Denver in the
summer for two months; the best two months of the year for
me.

Getting back to my uncles they hated my first name as
much as I did (though I think they liked me even less; but
did their duty). They also felt that I had come out of
nowhere so they nicknamed me Stray and it stuck; that's
what most of the cops on the force called me. Aunt Louise
was the only one who ever called me; by my first name.
Aunt Louise had recently retired to a small town called
Driftwood Colorado and I wished she had been closer
especially when I had run into the wall of blue at my job.
Cut to today as I told you earlier I'd taken a new job as the
sheriff in Driftwood Colorado.

As I drove to the Sheriff station; I saw that the downtown
area was newly painted but other parts were decrepit and
rundown. Stores had been closed and signs had been posted
that said for rent but the places looked like they hadn't been
rented in a long time. The back alleys showed signs, of
hookers working their wares with discarded condoms.

The town was surrounded by trees; but the main source of
jobs in the past had been lumber and the company had
pulled up stakes and moved away. Factories and brickyards
were closed. Some of the homes have seen better days and
the downtown core was eerily quiet, with vacant storefronts
lining the streets. Crime which in the past hadn't been a
problem was suddenly up and maybe that's why the Sheriff
had quit? But that was the reason I was here. I'd shape this
town into a town we could all be proud of again if the re-
elected mayor could do as he promised and bring in the
jobs. I wanted to be happy here.
I'd just dropped off my three year old daughter with my
Aunt Louise. Stella Marie, my daughter seemed okay with
the new place and Aunt Louise; but was I? Aunt Louise was
sixty years old and a retired school teacher. Why was I so
worried? First day jitters obviously. Aunt Louise had my
back. She knew what idiots her brothers really were and
how they valued their friendships even more than family.
Being a single father I needed her more than ever.

Aunt Louise had urged me to apply for the vacant job of
Sheriff after hearing about my troubles as a cop in a suburb
of Halton, Illinois. I don't want to get into those troubles
right now. Today was a new day and I decided it was going
to be great even if it killed me. Just kidding! I was not
going to get killed like my dad had on the first day of the
job. Nerves were getting to me.
Sure it was hard settling into a new place for a child. A little
voice worried that I had made a mistake; but this was a new
start for both of us we should be happy. A month ago I had
been offered my dream job, Sheriff of a small municipality
in Driftwood, Colorado. Driftwood looked to me like a
small town of three hundred people where I'd be happy
raising Stella-Marie.

The streets were tree-lined; the cookie cutter houses had beautiful floral displays out front. The lawns were immaculate green and lush. Children rode their bikes up and down the streets with no fear of predators or gunplay. The people had seemed friendly and warm when I came for my interview for the job. What more could we want? I'd thought.

I'd done my research; but nothing had prepared me for the men all walking out on me. I stepped into the Sheriff's car. This blue flu wouldn't do! I knew from the dispatcher that the other cops were not happy with my appointment; but damn it was my first day on the job and they had a duty to serve and protect the citizens of Driftwood.

How could the four deputies just not show up for the day? Calls to their residences had gone to voice mail so they were even avoiding talking to me. I had to put my foot down hard or the men would never respect my leadership. I'd already faced a wall of blue in my old job; people pulling out the old politics line and drawing in ranks on the thin blue line. I'd wanted a new start to change the harassment I'd faced in my not so fair city over the last three years.

A bit of a long story which we'll get into later but suffice to say the line in blue was put up against me; simply because I stood up to another cop who committed a crime.

Driving down the road to go to my new deputy's home I grew angry. Hadn't I been through enough of this crap from the guys in Halton? I had been harassed day and night by those assholes.

I had to pull myself together; anger would not solve this problem. I could show them I was in charge but approachable. I was an outsider, hired on line. Hell I hadn't even met any of this guys but I would get along with them they just had to give me a chance. No that sound desperate and I wouldn't be that anxious. I would be the best Sheriff and boss they ever had.

I parked the squad car and mounted the wooden steps on the house. I knocked lightly on Deputy Gregory Barnes door. No answer. I gave it my best thundering police knock and the door swung open of its own accord. I pulled my service revolver and entered the residence wily. A smell of dead berries and apples entered my nostrils. I felt in my pocket and swished my menthol medicated lip balm under my nose. My adrenaline kicked in and suddenly I felt exhilarated and hyper aware.

I followed the putrid odor to a bedroom and found the late Greg Barnes with two bullet wounds to the heart surrounded by a dried rusty brown pool of blood. He'd been there at least two days. Nothing was disturbed in the home. No overturned furniture, nothing seemed out of place. He lived alone; so no help there. Was it a rogue girlfriend? Why was he dead?

What the hell? The first day on the job and my deputy is murdered? I needed those other cops that hadn't come to work today to help me solve this murder. Damn them and their blue flu.

I made the call to the coroner who was on call for autopsies. Then I secured the scene and called in the neighboring counties police force on loan until I could find my police force.

Less than an hour later, I had two officers, Alfred Jones and Paulo Scarlatti, I sent to the two of them to retrieve the first officer Joseph Paciocco on my list. Imagine my surprise when he called back to tell me that my other officer, Joseph Paciocco was dead too. Two shots to the heart and it looked like the same felon. Was I going to find all my missing officers dead?

A quick search of the other residences found all of the bachelor cops dead shot the same way. The family men with their families at home were dead too; but so were all their family members. They had all been shot with one shot to the head in their beds. They had not stood a chance. This was a professional job as each scene had been carefully scanned and nothing was left to find in the way of evidence other than the blood and bullets.

All in all the dead were Gregory Barnes, Joseph Paciocco, Jack Abrahams, Paul Jones, Harold Jones and his wife Cheryl, their two children Gail, and Fred, Vincent Vecchio and his wife Paula Antrim (both cops on the force), their baby, Adrian a newborn was alive in his crib and was taken into custody of the Children's Aid until a relative could be reached. Also dead were Robert Di Salvio and his wife Rebecca and their fifteen year old son William and their daughter Helen eight years old, Kas Mahmoud his wife Dayita, and their three sons, Aaban, Aahil, and Aatif ages five seven and nine.

What in the hell was going on? Someone had killed whole families. Why? Did they know something someone didn't want them to know? Was it retaliation?

This meant looking into backgrounds and finding out things people didn't want you to know. Being sheriff didn't make for a popularity contest in any case but this would have to be handled very delicately.

The police officers on loan couldn't continue to investigate this; I only had a temporary loan of their services for today. Even if I wanted to investigate I had to have help. I needed to call the FBI pronto and I knew just the guy my former partner Gordon Chum.

I dialed Gordon's number by heart. He answered on the first ring asking me about the new job and then said he'd speak to his boss and get the okay to bring a team down as soon as possible.

Meanwhile I was trying to comfort the staff left at station and ducking calls from reporters from all over the country and residents of Driftwood who were demanding to know what had happened. I took deep soothing breaths…Gordon would be here soon we'd get to the bottom of this. Penny Ambercrombie the office dogsbody and police dispatcher took charge and hustled the troops off to their stations to work on the tasks I'd given them.

Penny was tall and lean possibly one hundred and ten pounds though it was hard to tell for her clothes hung on her in non-descript browns that did nothing to enhance her looks and she was well over five feet eleven. Her hair was a rich chestnut and was wound tightly at the nap of her neck into a bun. Her eyes were her most striking feature that not even her terrible clothes sense could hide as they were a glittering emerald green that showed immense interest and intelligence. She appeared to be in her late twenties though her skin was leathered with the weathering an outdoors enthusiast had.

I could see that Penny was an asset to me and the sheriff's station in my job. But first I needed to call Aunt Louise and Stella- Marie and hope my daughter wouldn't get too upset that daddy would not see her until tomorrow at the earliest.

I picked up the phone and called the number by heart. There was no answer. Where could she be I wondered? My question was answered in the next few seconds by my office door swinging open. There my Aunt Louise stood with Stella Marie. Aunt Louise demanded, "Gunnar is it true? Are they all dead?"

The next thing that happened was three year old Stella-Marie jumping in my arms and saying "Daddy, I missed you."
I closed my office door no sense in putting on a show to the remaining troops and I hoped no one had heard my aunt utter my first name. Stella-Marie took the chair nearest me.

"I want an answer Gunnar."
"Not in front of the c.h.i.l.d."
"Ch.. i... ld, child, that's me," my precocious daughter answered.
"Stella-Marie already knows all about this. She turned on the television while I was in the bathroom and she heard about all your deputies and their families being found dead. She insisted I bring her here."
"Then you both know what I know. I'm investigating and I've called in the FBI."
"Daddy, are you safe? In that movie with the Kung Fu guy they tried to kill him and then killed his family," Stella-Marie answered.
"What have you been watching?"
"I remember his name. I love Jean Claude van Damme movies," Stella-Marie stated.
"Me too, pumpkin and we're safe. I haven't been here long enough to be mixed up in whatever is going on here," I reassured.
"You'll find the bad guys?"
"Daddy will find them. That's what daddy used to do before he had you," I answered.

"Be careful," Stella-Marie said with adult wisdom beyond her years.

"Stella-Marie is correct. You need to stay safe."

"I promise both of you, I will stay safe."

"We'll trust you."

"Can we have dinner together, daddy?"

"Of course we can my apple dumpling."

"I'm not an apple dumpling."

"No you're my little pumpkin."

"You're silly, daddy."

"What would you like for dinner? Pizza? Chinese food?"

"Pizza! I want pizza!!"Stella-Marie chimed.

I ordered her favourite Hawaiian pizza and we forgot work for a few minutes as we ate. Stella-Marie told me about her day between bites. Stella-Marie sounded happy and adjusting well to living in this new place. She didn't seem too worried about my job anymore. She kissed me goodbye and said, "Get'em, daddy. See you tomorrow, nighty, night."

I breathed a sigh of relief my daughter seemed happy despite all that was happening. I was the new sheriff so the danger to me from who ever committed these murders must be minimal if any, so my family was safe. Still I told Aunt Louise to keep Stella-Marie indoors and keep the doors locked reporting any suspicious activity to me.

Gordon arrived a few minutes later, "I'm Special Agent Gordon Chum FBI," he said showing his badge then continuing he said, "I'm here to take over this case."

"No. You're not you're here to assist me and the good people of Driftwood."

"I am here to serve the people yes and if that means taking over the investigation in a town that has seen fit to kill all its police officers save one..."

"How dare you? This town is peaceable. There is a
perpetrator or perpetrators who have committed a heinous
crime but we will get to the bottom of this."
"You should have recused yourself Sheriff."
I heard Penny Ambercrombie gasp and then mutter under
her breath, "What a maniacal idiot and a kook to boot."
"No, shouldn't! This was my first day on the job. I was to
begin tomorrow but I thought I'd get in and do a little
paperwork first. I am imminently qualified to investigate
this. I hadn't even met these men or their families; but I
care very much about what has happened to them. They are
police officers and my squad. Every one of them is mine so
this crime was done against me and my family. Do you
understand?"
"I understand the feeling and I promise not to step on your
toes, Sheriff. My men and I are at your disposal in this
investigation. You are in charge. Perhaps we could discuss
the particulars before my colleagues get here?" Gordon
stated.
"Please follow me this way to my office, Special Agent
Chum," I answered.
"Call me Gordon," my pal offered.
"People call me Stray," I stated.

Gordon pretended to be shocked and lifted an eyebrow at
me. Penny looked at Gordon with disgust but went back to
the front desk of the station.

Gordon entered my office and shut the door, loudly.
Spotting the pizza he said, "That went well."
"Yes, it did. Did you see the dispatcher, Penny
Abercrombie craning her head and her ears to listen to
you?"
"I saw her when I came into the station. She was frowning
at you and giving you dirty looks when you weren't looking
like she didn't believe you belonged here."
"I noticed those looks all day," I answered.

"That should be the end of that you can thank me now. She is directing those looks to me now and I'll wager she'll spread all over town how you defended the honor of the dead."

"Thanks Gordon for the assist; but how will we can we keep up the lie?"

"We begin a new friendship," Gordon said calmly then continued, "I hope you saved me a few slices of that I'm starved and my team is checking into the No-Tell Motel down the street within the hour."

I smiled and nodded handing him a couple of slices. It was good to see my old partner again.

"You are staying with me and Aunt Louise aren't you?" I asked.

"Lucky for you or is it me they are limited space in this town to stay and of course this allows me to begin a new friendship with you. All my agents have taken up the last rooms in the motel so I'm grateful your aunt will put me up. You did ask her didn't you?"

"Didn't think I had to, you know Aunt Louise loves you."
Gordon raised another eyebrow.

"Fine I'll call her now."

I dialed and Aunt Louise answered her cell phone on the first ring. Aunt Louise said of course Gordon was staying here. I told her not to tell anyone we knew her and she agreed after I told her why. Then she said she had to go as she had pulled over to answer the cell phone.

"So it's settled?" Gordon asked.

I nodded.

"What a terrible first day on the job for you pal," Gordon commented, "Especially after what happened to you more than three and half years ago."

I thought back to what I had been through the last three and half years and I found myself reliving that chaotic time in my mind.
I'd been about eight years on the job in the city of Halton, Illinois, a cop, just like my dad and grandfather and uncles before me. The city had gone to the gangs. . It was two steps and one step forward. Every time we turned around; another shooting another victim of a drive-by. Just the other day the victim was a seven year old kid innocently riding their bike! Luckily the kid lived; but we actively hunted for the shooter or shooters. I should have took that as an omen seeing as my grandfather and my dad lost their lives in the police service, but I went merrily on my way doing my job not expecting my life to come crumbling all around me.

A routine call to a richer neighborhood for a disturbance started it all. The dispatcher didn't think to tell me it was a domestic disturbance and the man had a gun. I'm always careful in those situations; more careful then the average cop but if you don't know you can't take precautions.
I knocked on the door and announced myself and shots barreled through the front door grazing my forehead and tearing my knee apart. I burst through the door grabbed the shooter and he shot me again. That should have got me accolades and medals right? After all I was shot doing my job, but no, all of those rightly went to my partner, Gordon Chum. The third shot resulted in a thigh wound that almost made me bleed out on the spot if it wasn't for the quick work of my partner Gordon Chum securing the prisoner and belting my thigh. Okay, so I got a medal or two, but Gordon was the real hero. See why he was the first man I called when my force had been gunned down.

Gordon is a second generation Asian American. A good
looking fellow and kinder than most men, he speaks softly
and carries a big stick. People underestimating him rather
walk away unscathed. Gordon standing at five foot six
weighed roughly two hundred and ten pounds of pure
muscle. He knew every fight technique I knew and more.
He saved my life a time or two.

Gordon was arguably one of the best partners I've ever had.
Gordon saved my life after I was shot on duty and secured
the scene until back-up could get there. He also called for
an ambulance for me. I was carted off to a hospital where I
spent the next three weeks in intensive car being prayed
over by my fellow cops, and the rest of the city.
Whatever chits they called in with the big guy upstairs it
worked, I survived and I should have been happy about
that; but all I could think was I missed my moment I was
supposed to die like my dad and my grandfather before me
on the job. It wasn't that I was that different when I came
out of the coma. Okay, so I had a few scars inside and out.
My forehead now sported a scar that I could cover with
bangs and temporarily bum leg. The leg didn't seem to
want heal in fact at one point they threatened to take off my
leg; but good old Gordon helped me fight them on that and
the knee healed to the point I could walk on it. But it wasn't
good enough for work, at least not then.

Suffering from self-loathing (and yes a little post-traumatic
stress disorder, if I truly admit it); I began to be curt with
everyone closing myself off from everyone and everything.
My wife, Gina took the brunt of all of this. I was cruel to
her at every turn. When she came to visit I'd ignore her.

I knew I needed help from the police shrink but I couldn't accept or admit that I, the wonder boy actually had a problem. Gordon begged me to quit loathing myself so much and making everyone else around me miserable but I didn't listen. I was content to wallow in my anger and self-loathing.

Weeks went by and Gina seemed unhappy despite her forced saccharine with me. She gave me an ultimatum get help; or she would leave me. I decided I wanted Gina so I found a shrink of my own choosing Doctor Collins for his add in the Yellow Pages.

Doctor Collins turned out to be a woman.

Don't get me wrong she wasn't a fantasy (that blonde fantasy with legs up to here and hiding behind glasses); no she was more like your grandmother. Non-descript, her silver hair short and curled tight to her head. Her voice was soft and she always offered me milk and cookies before a session. I kind of felt weird at first like she was family and I'd never been all that chatty with family anyway. I had so much trouble talking at first that I'd just sit there and stare at the walls; but after a few sessions she got me to open up about my childhood and then finally about the shooting. I began to feel better and worked on getting my knee back in shape so I could return to work.

I had a routine and I followed it. Therapy followed by afternoon sessions of psychotherapy. With the drugs Doctor Collins prescribed and all our talks I began to almost feel normal again. Okay, so I'm lying; I still had a few stray thoughts that I was a failure and that I should have died; but I labored hard to overcome them and worked on being nicer to my ball and chain. I even began to buy her flowers. As for my leg it was almost good enough to return to work.

Doctor Collins had scheduled my appointment for two p.m. on a Friday and I had looked forward to getting it over with and going home to surprise Gina. A cop buddy had offered me his family cottage and I planned a trip to the Poconos for the next week. I'd already called Gina's work and got her the next week off. It would be a fantastic surprise for her and a chance for us to just lay back and enjoy our weekend. I could even cook all the meals that I caught from the lake as it was loaded with fish.

I decided to change my appointment and let Gina know that it would now be at noon instead of two p.m... Surely I could charm my shrink into seeing me earlier and if not well then I see her next week after my trip. I arrived at the doctor's office to find a note on the door. It seemed my shrink. Doctor Teresa Collins had died suddenly this morning and they were rescheduling. A number to call followed the announcement.

Died! And all they thought about was their schedule? Devastating and only then realizing how close I had gotten with my shrink I fell to the floor crying and took about a half- an -hour to recover enough just to pull myself together. I told myself over and over everything would be okay but I didn't really believe it.

Enough of this shit!! A little therapy and I turned into a wimp; who cried at the drop of a hat. I was a Bullet and we were strong manly types; made of steel not mush!! People died!! Get over yourself I admonished myself. I had a life... a wife who loved me despite myself. It was time to man up and be the husband she deserved. I just had to get away with Gina. I'd go home and surprise her now.

Stopping at the gas station to fill-up and walking into pay I spotted roses. I picked some up and thought how pleased Gina would be. She deserved this after all I'd put her through the last two months. She'd surprised me two weeks ago, telling me that she was pregnant. I was overjoyed looking forward to our baby coming in six months. We had a new beginning and I would make her as happy as Gina had made me.

I thought about the look on her face; her joy at our baby and decided to book her favourite restaurant before we left town. We could then leave at nine p.m. I'd drive all night and we reach there by morning. It could be done despite my gimpy leg. Okay so I lied, I wasn't fully recovered; but soon I would be. My physical therapist was pleased and said I might even be able to go back to work in a month.

I went home opening the front door with my key and... You know what happened? It was that other old cliché...husband comes home and finds his wife naked doing the tango with another naked man.

I didn't recognize him from the back as he jumped out the window, naked clothes in hand. She could tell me who he was in her own good time. And I had plenty of time as I seethed and wanted to kill him but not her. I didn't want to hurt her at all I just wanted to take her in my arms and make this go away.

I took huge breaths and then realized it takes two to tango. I had brought this on with neglect and coolness towards her when all she did was support and love me. I took deep breaths to calm myself and rationalized. I was sure this was just a one-time thing.

I'd heard women could get quite horny in pregnancy I obviously had let her down.

I had been a terrible husband moody brooding, distant and angry. Gina deserved better and I could forgive her this. Couldn't I? Sure I was angry, but I would never harm Gina despite my thinking for her lapse in judgement. I had stared at her five foot nine naked figure with its well-endowed breasts and tiny waist and wondered how she hid our baby in it.
Her curly black hair fell in ringlets to her waist. I realized I loved her. I loved our baby. It had been my neglect that had driven her to this; I was prepared to forgive her and take her on my planned trip. We'd been married fifteen glorious years, okay so not glorious, fiery but she was also pregnant and I wanted my child to have a stable home with two parents one of them me. I'd been spared so my kid could grow up with a dad it was as simple as that.

I told Gina all of this and she laughed. It seems that she and her paramour had been carrying on since day one of one of our marriage. Once more she had an amniocentesis last week and received the results this morning the baby was his not mine. I was devastated all those dreams of playing catch with my daughter. Taking her to daughter and daddy dances. Having her look up to me, with hero worship came crashing down. Yes, I know it could have been a boy; but I had my heart set on a girl.
I admit it I went against all my principles and begged her to stay and claim the baby was mine. We were married so the baby was legally mine. She laughed that twinkly laugh that I knew so well and I had to restrain myself from retaliating as she told me she already left me I just hadn't noticed. Gina said she was tired of living a lie. Now that I knew it was all out in the open and she file for divorce and move in with him. She lunged at me slapping me and asked why could I be like him?

I want to hit back at her but I couldn't if I it back I wouldn't be any better than the men I arrested who abused their wives.

Why couldn't I be like him? The man that she slept with, she raged. I was stupefied and getting angrier by the moment I knew I needed to leave before I regretted losing my temper; but I needed to know who had replaced me.

She laughed again and said I find out soon. I begged her to tell me and she did.
HIM? I fell to my knees. How could it be him? No, it wasn't Gordon Chum; but someone else I considered a friend and brother. Gordon wouldn't do that to me. The dirty dog who had betrayed me had been a partner, a mentor and good grief the man was old...fifty five if he was a day and close to retirement.
Why had she cheated on me with my former partner Derek? He'd broken the cop code you didn't sleep with another cop's wife. He'd slept around I heard how many women he'd been with had she? I told her and she laughed telling me it was his cover story. She continued snickering and said at least every woman didn't try to pick him up in front of her. She packed her bags and then trounced out the front door to join him at his house.

I thought I could handle it all and maybe I could have if she hadn't come back a half an hour later saying she'd changed her mind. She stripped to her skivvies and begged me to change her mind. What's a hot blooded male to do? I wanted to prove I was the better man, the better lover, so I turned my back and began stripping too.

That's the last thing I remember before waking up in hospital. How I got there and what happened after that I couldn't recall until much later.

The doctor kept speaking to me but it sounded like gibberish. My brain didn't want to understand. I don't know why. I closed my eyes, but before I drift under I hear them talking.

"Will he be okay now, doctor?" Gina asked.
"We'll know better when he answers my questions," I perceive the doctor say far away.

I heard footsteps as someone left.

A voice I recognize as Gina whispered in my ear, "You stupid son of a bitch. Why didn't you die? You'll wish you had now."
I struggle to wake before she can harm me but it's like moving under quicksand. I hear an alarm sound and footsteps run into the room.

"What did you do you now, you evil bitch?" I heard Gordon yell as I feel myself falling through layers of unconsciousness into nothingness.

~0~

Please look for this book June 2017

Excerpt from a Penny Saved A Murder Earned- Chapter 1 – Bloody Shoes

"A penny saved is a penny earned" ~ Benjamin Franklin

The blood streaked across the floor, but he had carefully sidestepped it. Stupid bitch! She got what she deserved. How dare she defile his Angel's property? He hadn't left a trace...had he? No, he was too clever by half.

A voice he didn't recognize interrupted his thoughts, "I didn't spot you entering. Working late, dear? Of course, I forgot; you have an early opening tomorrow."

The man strode closer to the killer and the body lying on the floor, "Wait a minute, you aren't the lady. Who are you? You shouldn't be here," the man continued clearly alarmed.
"You shouldn't be here either," the murderer insisted.
"You, you killed Megan. I'm telling."
"Really? You know this was something you shouldn't be allowed to see."
"I'm leaving. I didn't notice anything," the man lied, witnessing the blood.
"I'm sorry pal. Wrong place, wrong time!" the killer answered.

The homeless man ran dodging racks, finally deciding to hide behind some shelving. The killer ran after him, puzzled for a moment because he could see no trace of the homeless person. The murderer then laughed, as he realized how foolish the vagrant was being, his stench gave him away. He subdued the man with a Taser gun. Waiting seconds he then pulled the man from his hiding place. Taking ties from within his pocket; he fastened the man's arms and feet. Satisfied that the homeless person was now trussed up like a turkey, he smiled.

"P...P....P...Please! I don't want to die!" the man cried, visibly sweating and starting to shake.

The man tried to kick out his legs and arms but failed.

"You've heard about fate? Well sorry but this is your fate, buddy!" the murderer explained.
"P...P...P...Please, I'm begging you! Couldn't you let me go? I won't tell! I'll move to another city. Besides who would listen to a homeless man?"
"Someone would. My Angel would."
The homeless man then smiled as if to gain trust from this killer, "You won't hurt the lady who owns the store, will you?" he asked.
"I would never harm my Angel. How dare you?" the killer responded outraged.
"S...S...S...Sorry! I didn't mean to insult you! Please just let me go. I'm harmless ask anyone...."
"What is your name?"
"Why do you need my name?" He asked looking puzzled then reconsidering he answered, "My name is Al."

The killer put his gloves back on and smoothed them and then turned his back on his victim.

"You're going to kill me now. Aren't you? Just don't harm the sweet lady who owns this store. Will it hurt?" the man asked resigned.

"I would never hurt my Angel. She is sweet isn't she? Unfortunately that also makes unscrupulous people take advantage of her."

"I promise I would never take advantage of her kindness. I wouldn't!!! She's the best part of my day and this city, Happy Valley, Ontario. She picked me up from the gutter and helped me."

"I know you wouldn't and it hurts me to do this. Tell you what though, I'll make your death painless because I like you, Al," the killer offered, feeling suddenly sorry for the man. Then he checked himself. Living on the streets was hell; maybe he was doing the guy a favour? Yes, of course he was. Taking a pill bottle out of his pocket and opening the dispenser, he placed some in a coffee cup he took from the sideboard. He filled the cup with the tepid coffee from the coffee pot, stirring the pills in rapidly.

"C...c...c...couldn't you let me go? I won't tell and I'll watch over her when you're not here."

"Sorry, times up, Al. Here now, drink this coffee," the assassin commanded placing the mug at Al's lips.

Al tried not to drink and spit some of the coffee out, but the assassin plugged his nose and the cup was soon empty.

"Admit it Al, you had a crappy life. Just give in and go to the light. I hear good things wait there for people like you," the killer stated.

Al tried to fight some more, but he soon found it was losing battle. Al's breathing slowed as he slipped into a deep sleep and stopped breathing altogether. His age and living on the streets made the pills work fast.

Now what to do with the body? The killer thought. His Angel must not find this man's remains here, bad enough he left Megan's body here for his Angel to find. He couldn't hide Megan though she needed to be found. Every needed to know she suffered for her crime. Maybe even his Angel would see Megan's evil and protect herself from people like that. This man, Al however knew his Angel and she cared about him. It was so like her to look after the homeless. He could let her cry over Al. Where could he put the man so he wouldn't be found?

The dumpster of course...the perfect place for Al! The day after tomorrow was garbage day. Covered in garbage no one would find Al.

~0~

The next day
Lily

Ominous clouds replaced the morning's sunlight turning the skies to shades of deep purple and navy blue, streaked with gray. Lily Kelly stared at the sky for moment, and then departed the courthouse doors in Happy Valley, Ontario, Canada, skipping down the steps. The city looked its age of over a hundred as the buildings downtown looked old and decrepit. If only the town could find some money to fix downtown Lily thought.

Then her mind turned to Amelia, her cousin and best friend. Amelia needed Lily to support her in her grief. Lily had a fight with her husband Horace again this morning about how much time he was spending at the office and how much time she spent supporting Amelia. Lily was always working, and so was Horace, so how much time was Rose their fourteen year old daughter really getting?

Lily had won in court, but all she could think about was her family. Everyone needed her and she felt like she was being pulled in three different directions. Something had to give and it looked like it was her job. She would have to cut back on some of her work. Her family had to come first.

Lily stumbled some more over the steps only stopping from hurrying across the courtyard to her office, when her heel broke on her shoe. Today was supposed to be about her victory after her win in court; but it appeared with her expensive shoe's heel breaking, she was mistaken. They ought to get the ruts in the paving stones fixed; that was her reflection as she cursed her bad break. What did they say about omens? Maybe she should have taken a hint from the heavens' darkening? She noted as her bad luck had seemed to get worse with the arrival of some reporters.

"Ms. Kelly, give us a statement about the Rockwood case?" yelled one reporter.
"Ms. Kelly, how does the Sulimani family feel about your victory?" yelled another.

One bold reporter stepped forward, "Crown Attorney Kelly, congratulations on your win. Was it hard to try a case which involved a council member?" asked Paul Knight from the local television station, thrusting a microphone in Lily's face.
"Anyone who commits a crime in Happy Valley will be tried by the Crown with the full force of the law, despite their office. So no, I did not find it difficult to do my job," Lily replied testily.
"Thank you, Ms. Kelly. What does the Sulimani family think about the judgement?"

"Amani Sulimani was five years old, when Zebadiah Rockwood's truck went through a red light. His truck struck the back of the Sulimani's SUV killing her. He then left the scene pursued by good Samaritans, who wished to stop Mr. Rockwood from continuing driving drunk: a pursuit caused by Mr. Rockwood's actions, which put a number of lives in danger."

"Will the family be comforted with this conviction?" queried another reporter.

"Amani Sulimani existed as their only child. Mr. Rockwood's conviction will not bring her back, but hopefully will bring some peace of mind to her family knowing he will be behind bars." Lily answered.

"Do you sense, given your own personal tragedies that you'll be able to get a sentence fitting the crime?"

"My family's history does not come into my trial cases, only the person's guilt."

"And when will sentencing take place?" asked another reporter.

"Sentencing will take place next month."

"Thank you Ms. Kelly. This is Paul Knight reporting, with an update on the Zebadiah Rockwood's drunken driving case. Zebadiah Rockwood was a long time council member here in Happy Valley. He took a leave of absence to deal with his legal issues. Mr. Rockwood was charged with impaired driving causing death, two counts of failing to remain at the scene of an accident and dangerous driving last December. When asked about the conviction today Mr. Rockwood and his lawyer issued a no comment. We will have the complete story for you at six pm. Paul Knight reporting for CHPV-TV."

Lily hated speaking on camera, even though it was part of her job as the Crown attorney, so she was glad the scrum had been completed.

She hated sounding tough and unyielding but it was all in the description of her job title. She had fought difficult challenges to get this job and she had to work hard and fight hard to keep it. After all there were aspects of her job her she loved like putting the bad people that would harm others away. The press was gone and she was now free to go to her office to file her reports and leave early. She crossed the street, entered her building and went straight up to her office.

"Victory is mine!" Lily Kelly cried triumphantly as she walked into her office.

"So you won?" asked Colleen Finn, her administrative assistant.

"Yes, I bested that idiot, Michael Taylor. He thought he would beat me in court. He actually believed his client would win."

"Good for you, boss, I knew you would nail his lily white ass to the wall. He's such a scumbag lawyer all his clients seem to be as guilty as hell."

"Colleen! Language! But thank-you," Lily answered, showing pearly white teeth.

Colleen looked expectantly at Lily and she felt stupid did she miss something? Oh the joke! Lily hadn't laughed at Colleen's wit.

"Funny, I got it. Zebadiah Rockwood's sentencing takes place next month, but he will be held until then; no bail, no goodbyes to his favourite watering hole. As the Crown, I'll recommend the longest sentence I can get that he can serve. It's victories like these which make my job worthwhile. I don't know how much satisfaction this will give that little girl's family, but at least they'll know her killer remains in jail. He can't take another life again, because he will be incarcerated."

Lily went over to her desk and sat down.

"Can you imagine Michael Taylor, tried to use the defence that Rockwood was not drunk. Just tired? He claimed Rockwood drank only after the accident, while driving his company's truck; so the company couldn't possibly be responsible,"

"I believe you told me that before," Colleen commented, "However I'm glad you proved he'd drank so much before getting in the truck. That proved he was legally under the influence when the accident occurred. I hope I was some help in that aspect."

"Yes, you were invaluable."

"Thanks, Lily."

"It's still early; only nine forty-five, and my day's clear until what, two-thirty?"

"That's correct." Colleen replied.

Colleen checked a day planner, frowning, "Is everything okay, Lily? You seem a little down."

"Everything is fine. Amelia's grand opening starts at noon, but I promised to be there sooner if possible. If I go right now, I'll surprise her," Lily grabbed her coat to leave.

"I'm glad she's doing so well. Although after what happened, Amelia needs the encouragement. Please tell her, I'll try to get to her store another day. I hope her store has great success."

"Thank-you, I will tell Amelia. Hold all my calls Colleen. Unless it's urgent then call my cell."

"I'll do that. What time should I say you'll be back?" Colleen responded to a departing Lily.

"Tell whoever asks that I'll be back after two p.m..."

"And if they ask where you are?" Colleen questioned.

"Tell them I'm meeting with a witness," Lily replied with a wink.

"If there's cake bring me back a piece. Please, boss?"
Colleen begged.
"I ordered a cake, but it's not supposed to arrive until one
thirty so we'll see. I'm leaving now. Remember only urgent
calls to my cell phone." Lily cautioned, leaving through the
front door.

She twisted her shimmering brown hair back up into its
traditional bun. Pulling out her cell phone, she dialled
Amelia's store. There was no answer. How odd! Amelia
must be busy putting out last minute stock.

~0~

A few minutes ago

A lone male walked into the store. His left hand held a gun
while his right hand steadied it. He strode in with caution.
His dark brown eyes dart from corner to corner, searching
for an assailant. His well over six-foot tall frame slouched.
Ruggedly handsome, with dark brown hair clipped short to
his head; he was dressed in a dark blue jacket and dress
pants; a badge is also clipped to his belt buckle. Finding the
scene secure he putting his gun away and pulled a pair of
gloves out of his suit coat pocket and a pair of booties,
which he slipped on his shoes.

He checked the victim. No pulse. Advancing forward, he
bent down to check the second woman; her phone still in
her hand, her head bloody. He noted the second victim was
still breathing, though unconscious. He looked around, as if
waiting for someone. Deciding they weren't coming yet, he
took out a mini recorder. He started scanning the scene and
speaking aloud.

"This is Sergeant Detective Emmett Rogers. I am at the
scene of a homicide, at Quirks, one forty five Maple Street.
A woman lays sprawled out across the floor. The woman's
arms are positioned underneath her, as if to break her fall.
The back of her head and her long blonde hair are streaked
in rusty-brown blood, as well as her clothing below the hair.
Blood pools across the floor spiralling out in two long
streams. Footprints are noticeable, as if someone stepped
through the drying blood. The weapon appears to be a pair
of scissors, found beneath the victim. I have marked both of
these."

The man spoke aloud as he walked around, carefully
avoiding contaminating the evidence, by stepping over a
paper cup.

"A coffee cup... possibly one of those lattes is overturned.
I'm sure the forensics team can determine this if necessary.
Its contents are also spilled on the floor and countertop.
Coffee is spilled at the front door and possibly on the shoes.
The second victim's shoes are not on the bruised victim, but
on the floor. The shoes can be found near an overturned
ladder, at the front door. It appears the woman, who appears
unconscious, may have been carrying a ladder and toy stock
to place on the shelves, when she slipped in the blood.

The man paused to think.

"This might be a setup by the second victim to cover the actual crime. The woman, however, seems to have the victim's blood all over her clothes and hands like she crawled through the blood. I believe there are two possible scenarios here. One the owner of the shop, one Amelia Kelly (the unconscious person), murdered her employee or unknown victim and set this up to appear a perpetrator broke in and killed her accidentally hurting herself in the process. Or two... it is at it now seems that she stumbled on the crime scene and harmed herself."

He pulled out a notebook again and examined the room taking some more taking notes.

"Is it a robbery gone wrong? It is too soon to tell. The store owner will be en-route to hospital as soon as the EMTs have arrived. Interview to follow. The time is now ten twenty a.m.," he concluded turning off his recorder. He examined the room scribbling on his notepad.

~0~

Now
Lily and Detective Emmett Rogers

The man's eyes turn and his vision focused completely. A woman entered the store. His eyes took in her tall and slender form and her long shimmering brown hair, pulled into a tight roll. He noted she was closely followed by the Emergency technicians and gave a sigh of relief. The woman entering the store had brilliant blue eyes. He had a feeling she often turned heads, even dressed as she was, in her business attire. But he noted something about the way she walked screamed money and upper class.

"Oh no, Amelia!" she screamed and tried to rush to Amelia, but was stopped by the man's arm.

"This is a crime scene ma'am. We don't want you disrupting our evidence. Let the EMTs and detectives do their job. Then you can go to ...you're er...friend?" Sergeant Detective Rogers commanded.

"Crime scene? What has happened?" Lily asked politely, wanting to be cooperative.

"Ma'am, I'll know better after I assess the scene. Until then, please remain near the front door." ordered Detective Rogers briskly.

"I promise I'll stay out of the way; but at least can I get her Adrienne Changs?"

"What or who, are Adrienne Changs?" said Detective Rogers looking totally perplexed.

"Shoes, those shoes right there!" Lily pointed to a pair of heels lying behind the yellow tape.

"You're worried about shoes? Woman! Do you have any idea of what's going on here?" Detective Rogers snapped, shaking his head.

"You sexist pig!" countered Lily under her breath.

"Men!" Losing her temper now and louder she continued, "Those shoes are worth five hundred dollars! And she probably wore them for what a half an hour? And you want me to walk away and leave them to be destroyed in some kind of liquid!"

"Liquid that's blood! And five hundred dollars for shoes? Is she crazy?" Detective Rogers asked dumfounded.

"No! She's not crazy. How dare you?" Lily asked suddenly outraged.

He was smug wasn't he? Handsome yes, but oh so smug, she questioned herself. That wasn't important. Amelia was injured on the floor and he questioned her? Instead of letting her go to her cousin! What was wrong with Lily? Why was she so worried and focused on the shoes? They were only shoes. Amelia was injured; who cared about footwear?

"Sorry, ma'am, the shoes are evidence now. Name? Occupation? Address?" Detective Rogers barked, ignoring her statement.
"I want to see your identification first, and then you'll get the information," insisted Lily.
"I am Sergeant Detective Emmett Rogers," the man revealed, showing his police badge.
"Oh that's funny," Lily uttered laughing, "If you and Amelia were introduced it would be Aem and Em."

Lily followed this up by hysterically laughing and then alternatively crying. What was wrong with her? She never lost it like this. She always appeared a professional. She had seen crime scenes. She could handle this. Couldn't she? Amelia would be okay. Wouldn't she?!

"Get a hold of yourself Lily. You have embarrassed yourself," Lily heard this voice in her head, she recognized as her father's. Odd how her Dad's voice, came back to her now, she rarely saw him, since he lived in Prague and he only called about twice a year.

"Ma'am, what you are saying is not remotely funny. Are you all right? Put your head between your knees if you feel lightheaded. I think your friend's relatively fine. She might have a head injury and possibly a broken leg, but she'll be okay." Sergeant Detective Rogers then turned to the Emergency technicians (EMTs) to seek confirmation demanded, "Right?"

"Should be. But head injuries can be serious," the one EMT replied.

Sergeant Detective Rogers shot him a disapproving look.

"Yes, the Sergeant Detective is right. She'll be fine. She'll be taken to the hospital for treatment," the Emergency Technician agreed, finally.
"See...what did I tell you? Now that we have that out of the way; I need to see some identification and then get some answers to my questions. Name? Address? Occupation? The reason you are here?" Detective Rogers barked at Lily.
"Amelia's my best friend and more. This should have been the greatest day of her life, her opening of her new store; a one of kind toy and collectibles retailer. A grand opening and now it's ruined. Who did this to her?" Lily asked, uncharacteristically wringing her hands and still trying to regain her calm, as thoughts of Amelia's demise threatened to enter her mind.
"Ma'am, she slipped in blood. She hit her head on the floor and on the ladder. No one harmed her. She did this to herself," explained Sergeant Detective Rogers.
"I realize she's clumsy, but she didn't put blood there to trip in," defended Lily angrily.
"No, the blood was spilled by whoever killed the woman behind the counter."
"Someone is dead behind the counter?" Lily responded shocked and surprised.
"No comment; as I explained Ma'am this is an active crime scene. Now as I asked before what is your name?" Detective Rogers insisted forcefully again.

"Lily Kelly-Brooksfield. My husband is Horace Brooksfield, the mayor. We live down the street on Beaconfield. Do you want the number? It's nine hundred and sixty-two." she replied condescendingly.

"If you're Mayor Brooksfield's wife… then you're the Crown Attorney." Coming to this realization, Sergeant Detective Rogers hid a sigh.
"Please update me on this active crime scene, now," commanded Lily pulling back her shoulders.

Emmett Rogers put on his professional face and smiled. The smile was just so warm and inviting that Lily felt warm all over. Lily frowned back at him; she was just felt so angry. This cop who grinned back at her was the biggest reason. She was a married woman. She shouldn't be attracted to a cop who apparently existed to give her grief and solve a murder. She threw back her shoulders again. It was okay to look at someone attractive, she excused herself. Everyone looks, and most of the time it meant nothing. It's only if you acted on any attraction it became wrong. She would never act on the temptation. Besides he appeared to be the most annoying man she'd ever met.

"Ma'am, you know I can't fill you in on any of this case. You'll have to recuse yourself from this case, as you're familiar with the crime scene." Detective Rogers emphasized, once again interrupting Lily's thoughts.
"Why don't you just come out and say what you think. You consider me a suspect," Lily uttered.
"A lot of people are suspects in my book. I have to make a case for them committing the crime or I have to eliminate them as suspects. And don't attempt to solve this yourself; amateurs just get in the way." Detective Rogers explained, his eyes wandering.

Lily was slightly amused. Detective Rogers thought she wanted to insinuate herself into this murder investigation? She might not have before that comment, but she did now. He seemed to be focusing on Amelia or Lily as his prime suspect. Lily knew neither of them had committed this murder, so that meant she had no choice but to find out for herself who had committed this crime. She would pretend she wanted nothing to do with this situation, even as far as passing it off to her underling Barbara. After all she could always investigate behind the scenes.

Spotting the emergency technicians Detective Rogers exclaimed "Oh good, the ambulance has arrived to take the victim to the hospital. Now can we can get down to brass tacks; you can fill me in on these people and anything else you know or have held back from me."

"I want to go with her," Lily protested.

Lily pulled herself back taking several steps back putting distance between herself and this cop. It was odd, how alive she felt when she jousted with him. He was a cop investigating a murder and she was married.

"Stop this now Lily!" She told herself.
"Ma'am, I realize you want to go see your friend. Before I could release you from the scene, I need something from you. We need you to identify the other victim. Maybe you'll recognize her when I turn over the body." Detective Rogers explained, softening a little, as he slipped on another pair of gloves.
"Only if you'll stop calling me Ma'am. Call me Lily or Crown Attorney Kelly, but not Ma'am. It makes me feel eighty years old."
"If it will get you to identify the victim...thank-you Crown Attorney Kelly."
"Let's look, shall we?" Lily agreed.

Lily took a breath as she gathered herself to observe who lay there dead. She gasped as she stared over the counter to see the back of the woman's head. She covered her mouth in horror.

"Good grief! I never realized they appear so alike from the back," replied Lily shocked.

"Who do you think she looks like ma'am?" demanded Detective Rogers.

"What did I say about ma'am? Don't they give you sensitivity training at Police College? You want to know who this is? This is Megan, Megan Fowler. She's an employee of Amelia's. But she works evenings she's...is....was a college student. I can't believe this is Megan. Megan is such a sweet girl and worked part-time to be able to go to school and support her mother. Why would someone kill her? Do you think it's possible someone mistook her for Amelia?" Lily rambled, tears slipping from her eyes.

"That's a possibility, ma'am. We will explore all aspects."

"I know the drill, Sergeant Detective Rogers." Lily gave the detective a mock salute, "Why can't you admit that they mistook Megan for Amelia?"

"We don't have any of the facts yet, Ms. Kelly," replied Detective Rogers.

"What about Amelia? Is she in any danger?" asked Lily. "If I were to speculate, I suppose that could be a possibility," Detective Rogers answered non-committally.

They both watched as the technicians gathered the evidence and blood samples and took pictures before the body was taken away.

"Will someone be assigned to guard her and keep her safe?" Lily asked getting exasperated.

"That's in motion, Crown Attorney Kelly," Detective Rogers explained, trying not to sound annoyed that she's telling him how to do his job.

Detective Rogers and Lily turned as another cop swaggered into the store. Burly and well over six feet tall, his hair was dark like Detective Rogers. Unlike Detective Rogers, this man preened like a peacock; Lily was aware of the type. Guys like him smiled with their mouths and not their eyes. They thought all women should admire them and only them. She noted his smile went as far as his lips.

"What have you got here, Emmett?"

"Nothing you need to be concerned about, Brad," Detective Rogers replied, obvious tension showing between the two. "You should be able to get some great publicity out of this one," Brad said loudly to Detective Rogers.

Brad then strutted over to the murder scene.

"It's my case, Brad," Detective Rogers insisted.
"I'm not trying to interfere," Brad persisted walking around, "I just thought if you needed some help I would lend a hand. It doesn't look like something you could handle on your own."
"I don't need help, thanks, Brad. I don't need you messing up my crime scene." Detective Rogers declared "I've got it all under control.

"It doesn't look that way to me. I would solve this case quickly. You could use me in your corner," Brad continued. "We don't need you. Now the Crown attorney is here, so I have it all in hand. Goodbye, Brad." Detective Rogers practically spat.

"Ah, the lovely Crown attorney Kelly is here. Can't go now," Brad exclaimed trying to sound charming but failing miserably.

"And you are?" asked Lily putting her full aristocratic chill in to her voice.

"I'm Brad Owens, at your service, Attorney Kelly. Sergeant Detective Brad Owens. I use to be Emmett's partner," Brad explained smiling and pointing to Detective Rogers.

Detective Rogers rolled his eyes. "Thank God you're not anymore," He stated under his breath loud enough for only he and Lily to hear.

"So what do you think, Crown Attorney? Was it a robbery gone wrong?" asked Brad.

"I'm not sure. Why do I bother to tell you this? This isn't your case," Lily commented suddenly not willing to share with Brad.

She didn't know why. Something about his smile, and the way Emmett Rogers had reacted to him made her dislike him. Brad's smile was phony, like a used car salesman. It was slick and slimy. That wasn't fair to used car sales people. Lily was sure they were more honest than this phoney, Brad Owens. Lily had come across a lot of people in her job. She certainly felt she was a good judge of character. In fact, she could spot a phoney a mile away. Detective Emmett Rogers, unlike Brad Owens, appeared like he knew his job. She'd heard of him many times, but had never run into him on the job until today. Thank goodness for the Internet on her phone. He was a dedicated cop. He had done his time and had come up through the ranks, strictly on merit. Detective Rogers didn't seem to like Brad Owens and that was reason enough for Lily not to trust him.

Emmett Rogers had an exemplary record as a police officer; she trusted his instincts and knowledge over this smarmy, Detective Brad Owens. He'd get to the bottom of this. Lily wished he would let her leave soon and check on Amelia. They had spent their teen years together and were as close as sisters. She'd always felt responsible for Amelia, being two years older. She wanted to make sure Amelia was okay. "Okay. Well if you don't need my help, I'm leaving because I have work to do. There are other crimes to investigate." Brad answered leaving, "See you around Emmett."
"Not if I see you first," muttered Emmett under his breath.
"So am I free to go?" Lily demanded.

Emmett then offered her his pen.

"I have your address, so as long as you sign here in my notebook. "You are free to go," he said gesturing.

Lily glanced over at Detective Owens and watched him leave before reaching for the book. She then signed her signature with a flourish. Detective Rogers scanned the signature, thinking momentarily it was just as elegant as Lily. He shook his head, reminding himself to stay connected to reality.

"So I am free to go, Detective?" Lily repeated.
"I'll be checking in on your friend, of course, and I may need to follow-up with you later, but as of now, you are free to go." he smiled, already exhausted.
"I would expect nothing else from you, Detective Rogers."

As she got into her car, Lily breathed a sigh of relief she had finally been able to leave the store. She buckled up her seatbelt and put her car in gear.

Backing the car up, Lily pulled out into the street and narrowly missed getting hit by a car, she didn't view. Luckily the other driver slammed on his brakes. She noticed the male driver shouting, "Stupid woman driver" as she read his lips in her rear view mirror. He was justified in his anger. It had been her fault, but she didn't have time to dwell.

She headed down the road toward the hospital; despite her resolve her mind wandered. She thought about poor Megan's mother getting the news of her daughter's death. It would kill Lily to get news like that about her adopted daughter, Rose. What kind of monster kills a young woman? Why did, whomever it was, have to kill Megan? It wasn't a robbery, she'd read in Detective Rogers' notes, when he gave his notebook to her to sign her statement. As Lily drove, more questions flooded into her head. Was Amelia the real target? Megan certainly appeared like Amelia from the back.

Amelia didn't appear too hurt. Maybe she suffered a concussion? Concussions could be serious; she knew from her readings. The EMT hadn't said Amelia was in serious condition though. Not that the EMT could explain before Emmett Rogers got on his case. Revving the engine, she waited impatiently for the light to go green. Once Lily reached the hospital, she could reassure herself, Amelia was all right.

~0~

Excerpt from Dreams Can Kill ~ Chapter 1- Survival

The rain pelted down on me, as I struggled to come to my senses. My head felt like it had split in two, as if little lumberjacks had taken up residence. I opened one eye. The world spun sideways like a ride at the fair. I tried shutting one eye, then the other. I nearly fell back to sleep. I opened my eyes again, fighting the sleep which wanted to overtake me. I shuttered my eyes again, as my stomach protested. My whole body manipulated, bruised, bent and broken like some old rag doll discarded.

Sleep...sleep would solve my problems, my brain protested. No! I had a reason I needed to stay awake and alert...A little sleep, a part of me protested again. No, I must stay conscious. But I remained so tired. I dragged myself across the pebbled ground. My right leg stuck out at an impossible angle, obviously broken. I saw by lifting my head slightly and turning it that there appeared to be a road up ahead. I had to get to the road. If I dragged myself that far, surely I would be rescued?

But it was oh so hard, to drag yourself backwards, when you couldn't perceive where you were going. Oh no, what if he came back. He would finish me off...finish what he had started.

He who? Who was this person, who left me to die? Why couldn't I remember? Don't panic… the thing to do is right now is to reach help; then and only then would I be safe. I caressed large pieces of gravel which cut into the back of my head. I sensed I was close to the road. I reached out with my good hand and touched a paved surface. I knew I didn't have much strength left. I experienced the energy drain quickly leaving my body. I tried to fight the drain, but the world faded to black.

~0~

Chapter 2- Time Flies When You're Having Fun

I opened my eyes slowly. A tube appeared to have been inserted in my arm, feeding me intravenously, another tube down my throat as well. The lumberjacks in my head had been replaced by a dull achy sensation, as if I wasn't quite there. I suffered from weakness all over, but my body didn't have the same sensation, as when I had blacked out on the road.

My leg felt whole again and yet my leg didn't appear to be in a cast, or slung up on a tripod. How much time had passed? This definitely looked like a hospital room. The walls were pale white and I lay in a single bed. I rested in a private room how about that?

A nurse in a white cap entered the room. She grabbed my wrist and she proceeded to take my pulse. Alarmed, she stared straight into my face, "Well! Look who is awake. Welcome back to the real world," she proclaimed.
I tried to speak and realized the tube in my throat prevented that. Why was a tube in my throat I wondered? How long I been here? I assumed I looked scared because the nurse explained in a soft voice, "There, there honey, you take deep breaths, easy now."
"Why don't I go get the doctor? He can come and have a look at you and remove the tube from your throat."

I tried to nod my head in agreement but my head moved like lead. It seemed like eons before a man in a white doctor's coat appeared at my bedside. He appeared tall and lanky; with dark curly brown hair and warm deep blue eyes. Without any preamble he announced, "We will now remove this tube. Take a big breath now."

The tube came out as I gagged. Now I could ask the questions which plagued me.

"How did I get here? And where am I?" I tried to ask, croaking out the words, as if my voice hadn't been used in a while.
"Speak slowly. Here, have sips of water," answered the doctor.
"How did I get here?" I repeated, sure that I had been speaking clearer because I had taken a sip of water.
"I don't know who found you, but an ambulance brought you here in critical condition. You had a broken leg, some broken ribs, and a fractured skull."
"I came here in critical condition? So I've been here awhile?" I asked shocked.
"Yes, you've been here awhile. You were at a different hospital first. You are in Andrews' clinic now."

"Your condition appeared to be perilous there for some time. They lost you twice. We had placed you in a coma to let your brain swelling go away. Then we didn't know if you would ever come out of the coma."

He continued to explain like he couldn't quite find the words. But why would a doctor have trouble explaining a medical condition?

"I guess time flies when you have fun," I stated flippantly, hiding fear I didn't quite understand and becoming puzzled.

Why did he say first they then we? Hadn't he been there?

"I would like to examine you to see how you're doing now and get an update on your condition."
"I'm good. As you can see," I answered in response.
"I don't know if you even realize, but your speech isn't as clear as you think. You're slurring your words," he stated.
"I'm sure the words will come easier in time, but I'd like to check your reaction time and some other physical reactions."

What could he be talking about? I wasn't slurring my words. Was I?

The doctor began his examination. A flashlight flashed deep into my eyes. I blinked in response, as the light, so bright, made my eyes hurt. His response seemed to be to write down something on the chart, and pick up my wrist to take my pulse and blood pressure. He then listened to my chest with his stethoscope.

I moved my head and tried to sit up, but the effort zapped all my remaining strength. I surprised myself at how I felt like a newborn baby. He continued his examination. I grew tired but fought the sensation. If I closed my eyes for a moment, would the feeling would go away? I closed my eyelids and fell fast asleep.

I ran over hills. The night appeared so dark, and ink black; I could barely view two feet in front of me. My feet stumbled, as I tried to see the uneven ground in front of me. My palms clenched with sweat, as my heart pounded like the organ would jump out of my chest. I turned around, my eyes darting from side to side searching for my pursuer. No sign, but I knew he wasn't far behind.

My hair in a high ponytail, whipped at my face, as I picked up the pace in my flight. He seemed close enough, that I had the sensation of his breath on my neck... so close he might reach out and touch me. I turned again to see if I could glimpse him near, and I saw a man. But what puzzled me was what materialized in the man's face. Where his face should be, a gaping black hole yawned.

How could this be? The thought plagued me only for moment, as fear gripped me and survival instinct kicked in. Realizing if he caught me I would be killed, I ran stumbling over rock and uneven ground. When the inevitable happened, I tripped falling to my knees. He had me. There was no escape from my fate. I would die now. I struggled as he grabbed my left wrist twisting my arm.

This appeared no dream, I might awake from; he had me now and he would kill me.

I twisted slightly trying to free my wrist but he grabbed my other wrist and shook me slightly saying…, "Quite a dream you were having, but a dream none the less. Nothing can harm you now."

I stared into his face and slowly his look changed, from the faceless man, to another face entirely. This wasn't the man in my visions; the demon in my nightmare. I knew in my heart this remained an altogether different kind of man.

This face with smiling blue eyes radiated warmth, and kindness. His face stayed gentle, not violent. I had been dreaming and had mistaken his touch for the man in my dreams. I flushed with embarrassment.

"You are quite awake now? I won't harm you. Now, do remember me?"

I stared at him, slowly waking up, and realizing where I was.

"I'm your Doctor, Doctor Andrews, at your service, my lady. We met before when you awoke from your coma," he continued speaking softly, and gently, bowing at the waist and smiling.

Shouldn't I have recognized him immediately? Heat rushed to my cheeks, as I turned red in embarrassment.

I was a fish out of water. I didn't like the way I reacted; like something had happened and all was a secret to me. I liked to be in charge of my life every aspect, and right now it seemed like I appeared in charge of nothing.

"How long have I been here?" I whispered, trying to speak louder.

"I would have said it's a lot longer, than you think," he replied cryptically.

"Do you always answer a question with a question? I want an answer for my query," I demanded angrily.

"What do you remember?"

"I believe I asked you to stop making this an interrogation. If you must know, I remember waking up a little while ago the nurse came in and then you came a little later," I answered exasperated, wondering what could be wrong with me. I didn't get angry so easily. Did I? Why did I behave this way? Everything he said seemed to make me angry.

"Your little while ago was two days ago...," he explained, breaking off as if afraid to say more.

"But that's impossible..."

"You fell into a restorative sleep. It is not uncommon for patients who have been in a coma to do so."

"Two days? I slept for two days?" I commented incredulously.

"Yes," Doctor. Andrews stated.

"How long was I in a coma?" I asked worried to hear what he might say.

"What month do you remember?"

"You have to be in charge, don't you? Questions! Questions!" I replied, delaying the answer. I was suddenly afraid that I'd been in this coma far longer than I realized, and grew angrier.

"I know you're scared. Are you sure you want to know? The information can wait," he insisted.

"I'm not scared," I lied with false bravado, "I remember quite clearly the month is March."

"It is the eleventh of September nineteen hundred and seventy-one. Do you remember what happened the day of the accident?" he asked.

"That's not possible. I can't have been in a coma for six months. Why do you lie to me?" I spat at him.

"I know it's hard to assimilate but time has passed and it is September," he insisted softly, but firmly.

"Why do you persist in a lie? What do you have to gain with this preposterous story?" I demanded; still not ready to believe this.

"Exactly what do I have to gain? Sharron, I'm not lying to you," he stated sadly.

Until that moment I hadn't given any thought to my name, but as Doctor Andrews called me Sharron, I realized I wasn't even sure if that was my name. I didn't have a clue what my name was. My name might be Sharron, but I didn't recall the name. My name could be Mary, or Angela, or any other name in the world. If I had a surname, I couldn't remember it either. A huge blank spot stood where any recollection should be.

How could my last memory be of March, but I still had no recollection of my name, er names? This was normal after a long coma. I decided.

Perhaps my memory had been so underused, and only had temporary gaps? Or I was hungry? Yes, it had to be one of those things. A temporary aberration of the mind... No need for me to worry. No, need to share any such information.

My memory was only hiatus. That had to be the answer. Give it a few days and my memory would all come back. There was no need to tell the doctor, especially since my recollections would all come back. Absolutely not, I reasoned.

After all what good would it do to tell him? He'd look at me either with sympathy, or call in a shrink. I wanted none of the sympathy, and whispered glances which would follow. So I had a few memory gaps, nothing to worry about. It was perfectly normal after a coma, I reassured myself.

"What will you do with all this information Sharron?" asked Doctor Andrews suddenly concerned.
"I must admit the information was a bit of a shock to find the month was September and not March, but I'm over the surprise. "I'm hungry what does it take to get food around here?" I demanded, quickly changing the subject. Besides I was ravenous.
"I think you can start some light foods, some soft foods, Jell-O soup etc.," Doctor Andrews spouted. Turning to the nurse he commanded, "Nurse get a light meal for my patient."
"Certainly Doctor," the nurse replied, coming into the room rather quickly, at his summons.
Just when I thought I had successfully gotten rid of the doctor, he turned around and said... "I know you are rather tired and hungry right now, but I'm sure you to want to discuss these revelations later today."

How could I get him to change his track? I didn't want to discuss my memory loss with anyone. I wasn't ready for anyone to find out I didn't know who I was. If I told him, would he treat me like a mental patient?

No, I wasn't going to tell him, or anyone. I needed to fake what I remembered. They'd never know, I couldn't remember. I would then have the time to accept this myself, and hopefully everything would come back. No one would ever have to know.

Wait a minute, did he know, I didn't remember? He talked about the fact I'd been in a coma, but had he given me any knowing glances? I gave him a sideways glance. Deciding he didn't have a clue about my memory problem. I plotted to keep it that way.

"There is not a lot to talk about; but if you want to we can discuss my medical condition we can get to that later," I replied, hoping he would take my response as an agreement and leave.

Luckily for me he took the hint. Maybe he would even forget to come back and discuss this later? No, I hoped for too much, but he did look convinced that I'd talk to him later. Good then he'd go away.

"I will return later, Sharron."

He then left taking his questions with him. I breathed a sigh of relief. Now alone with my thoughts, surely I'd conjure up a memory or two. First I would eat and refuel. That would help the memories, as well as my stomach.

I stared at the food the nurse had brought in. I'm starving to death and the nurse gave me not enough food to feed a rabbit? I tried to pick up the spoon and found my hand wouldn't cooperate.

"Would you like some help?" the nurse asked kindly.
"I can do it myself," I responded stubbornly.

Although I had found it difficult to raise my hand to my mouth, that soon became easier. I found by clamping my hand around the spoon I could manage to feed myself. It was then I realized how much work I had ahead of me. The nurse watched, so I smiled at her like everything was fine. She smiled back and left.

I soon made short work of the food and wanted to move on to the therapy I recognized I needed. I would set the memories, or lack of them aside, and working on building up the muscle tone and abilities I'd lost. When the body restored itself, I would begin to remember. I understood without being told, that I had to begin like a baby to exercise my limbs and I wanted to start immediately. Let's be honest. I realized I could remember something. I grasped now that I was an impatient person, at least when it came to doing things I had to be doing. I called the nurse on the call bell to ask about therapy and exercises.

"Yes?" I heard a disembodied voice somewhere over my head say. Momentarily puzzled, I then realized the voice came from an intercom.
"Sorry to bother you but when can I start therapy? I need to get my limbs moving," I explained.
"Dear, you are barely out of coma. I'm sure your doctor would want you to build up your energy first. Or wait at least until you started solid foods."

She sounded surprised and had a hint of censor in her voice. No support there. I wanted those six months back, but clearly that wasn't going to happen. Move on, I told myself. I'd wasted six months sleeping, time to fight back and get back into fighting form as they said. But who had said that?

I somehow knew I was a fighter. I'd have to do everything myself; something I knew I always did. But how did I know that?

I thought about what would work, and what limbs need to work. My hands needed to a work out. Okay, they need to grip. How do you make hands stronger?

You give them something to grip. Squeezing something soft, medium soft, would work. Where to get something to work my grasp? I couldn't even get out of bed. My limbs were useless, absolutely useless. My hand shook in weakness, from forcing the stupid thing, to do its job and feed me.

All of this began to feel hopeless. ..No, I wasn't some stupid helpless female. I had to figure out a plan. You're on your own, I told myself, nothing new. You can overcome any odds. Think, Sharron, think!

How about some finger exercises? Slowly working each finger, and then in tandem, I would get back movement. I began the exercise I devised. It sounded so simple when I had thought of how to exercise the hand, but painful and tiring. Work through the pain, I told myself. Isn't that what you've always heard?

I forced myself to do the exercises for what seemed like hours, until I couldn't take the pain any more. Then I decided to exercise my arms. Gripping well enough to pull myself up to the bar over my bed, I reached I'm with my right hand to grab the pole. My fingers won't cooperate. My fingers are weakened and my grip slipped. Damn it! Even simple exercise was impossible.

"Nothing is impossible," a voice spoke loudly in my head. But whose voice did I hear? My memory had fled, if it was ever there. I only comprehended the voice had been someone I loved, and respected. Was this a father, or a father figure? I knew I was bone weary, and a great sea of lethargy stole over me. It would be counterproductive not to take a nap, I reasoned. Surely a short nap would restore my energy and I would begin again.

I closed my eyes soon I began dreaming. At first the dream appeared happy. I viewed myself in a beautiful home and grinning at someone I couldn't see.

I smiled and felt great joy, but the sky grew dark and I found myself outside on a field. The moon overhead slowly covered by clouds, and I grew terrified. Something was wrong. The faceless man chased me once more. I ran over rocks and streams and more rocks. He kept coming and coming. I knew he'd soon be on me. He nearly had me when I willed myself to wake up saying… This is a dream and I want to wake up now.

I awoke gasping for air like I had been running a marathon. A strange man sat by my bed. His hair appeared dark, practically black, greasy, and slicked back. He had black thick glasses that he peered over like they were a prop.

An oversized suit coat in plaid and matching pants completed the picture. Despite his harmless appearance, he struck terror to my heart. What gave me the idea he put on this persona, like a piece of new clothing? I think it was his face which seemed to give it all away, like he tried too hard to portray someone he wasn't.

As I gazed at him, he jumped from the chair he sat and exclaimed…"About damn time you woke up out of the coma Sharron. I thought you laze there forever."
He then continued, as if choosing his words carefully, "Oh Sharron, this is the most wonderful day of my life." Then he pulled me to him, fiercely.
"Let go of me, this instance. Who do you think you are? I said don't touch me! And quit acting and looking around there's no audience for your play," I blurted out, before I stop myself.

"Sharron that's not funny. Quit joking. You always had a wicked sense of humour, but I'm not laughing." the man stated, sounding annoyed and grabbing my wrist.
"I said let me go, and I meant every word. Now kindly take your hands off me," I demanded at the top of my lungs, struggling unsuccessfully to free myself of the grip, he now had on my wrist.

Taken back by my yelling, he let me go, but he still continued to treat me, like a bug under a microscope. Suddenly switching gears, his face changed. It was if a curtain went down over his face. He took on a concerned look and then a hurt look. I admit he nearly had me fooled.

I started thinking I had forgotten a boyfriend, but surely I wouldn't suffer from such bad taste.
He wasn't my type. He seemed quite violent too. I wouldn't have been so foolish to get mixed up with a weirdo like him! Would I?

"Sharron quit staring at me that way you're making me uncomfortable. I'm not amused here...Wait a minute you're not kidding .You don't recognize me at all. You don't recognize your fiancé?"

I recognized somehow that he was put on an act. No, I wasn't engaged to him. If I had been it would boggle my mind. He had to be lying, I decided. Why I didn't know, but I knew he lied.

I had no sparks with him. In fact something about him gave me the creeps. He repulsed me and made my stomach hurt. He certainly didn't sound sincere. He put on an act ... but why? He grabbed my wrists again, once again in a vice grip. I struggled valiantly, but his grip tightened and I couldn't handle his fierce clutch in my weakened stated.

"Let me go you, caveman. I don't know you and what is more, I don't ever want to know you," screamed at him fighting frantically.

"Sharron you cut me to the quick. Why do you say such things to me?" he whined, letting go of my wrist, but gripping my arms even tighter.

Maybe it was because of my dream, but suddenly I was terrified. Why did they leave me all alone with this crazy man? Where was everyone else? Couldn't they hear me shouting?

"Let me go. Let me go....Don't touch me," I yelled at the top of my lungs, and then screamed, hysterically "Help me someone help me."

As I started to pull harder frantically to be free he stilled held fast. What kind of evil demon had me in his grasp? I tried to bite him, but that was impossible; finally in the answer to my screams were footsteps running. Seconds later a nurse and Doctor Andrews entered.

"Let my patient go immediately. I said let her go," Doctor Andrews growled, pulling the man's arms behind his back. I breathed a sigh of relief. I was safe. Doctor Andrews had saved me.

"I wasn't hurting her! What kind of a man do you think I am? Gee, I have more bruises than her. She acted crazy, so I grabbed both her arms to calm her," the man explained, sounding plausible.

Surely Doctor Andrews and the nurse who followed him in, didn't believe his act?

"Your technique doesn't seem to have calmed her, but it certainly frightened her," Doctor Andrews said, checking my blood pressure and heart rate.

"You can't tell me what to do. She's my fiancée I can speak to her anyway I want," complained the man, loudly.

"You've upset my patient. Her blood pressure and heart rate is elevated as well. This is not good for my patient, so I can tell you what to do. What is your name?" demanded Doctor Andrews.

"Titus Brown is my name and Sharron is my fiancée," the man replied a little too quickly.

Doctor Andrews consulted his clipboard. He pointed to it and then announced, "This is the approved register and you're not on the list. Leave now, Mr. Brown, or I'll have security escort you out of the facility."

"I'm not going anywhere. Who do you think you are?"

Mr. Brown showed his true colours, I thought. They would trounce him faster than you could say Jack Robinson.

"Mr. Brown, so far I've been pleasant. The nurse has already called for a security guard. I suggest you leave now and don't come back, or you will find yourself with a trespassing charge and jail time," Doctor Andrews said through his teeth.

"I'll be back with my lawyer and you'll be sorry," Mr. Brown menaced.

Two security guards entered and forcefully removed Mr. Brown from my room. I began to shake like a leaf. I tried to stop, but I grew frightened. Someone had tried to kill me and that is why I was in the hospital. What if it was Him, Mr. Brown?

They wouldn't let him take me when he talked to his lawyer? Would they? Words I hadn't want to share, spilled out of my mouth, first in torments, and then at a screeching level.

"I don't know who the heck he is, but I do know I don't know him. I'm not his fiancée. Don't let him come back lawyer, or no lawyer. I don't want to see him. Someone did this to me! I wouldn't be surprised if the person was him!" I guess I appeared a little too hysterically and forcefully, because the next thing that occurred was Doctor Andrews plunged a needle into me.
"Please, please don't. It's not necessary, really. I'll be good," I pleaded too late.
"It's a little sedative. I don't like your colour, your blood pressure, or your heart rate. You've had a nasty scare and your body isn't able to cope with this right now. Calm down now," he said comforting "Go to sleep."
"I think I hate you," I replied vehemently.
"That's okay, you can hate me if you need to," he answered, smiling.

Damn him and his handsome smile! Something about the grin, made me want to smile back and tell him all my secrets.

"Don't leave me alone. He might come back," I pleaded as I drifted into a deep drugged sleep.

~0~

If you enjoyed Jack Be Nimble please consider leaving me a few words at your favourite retailer and if you liked the excerpts and would like to read more of my books please check out one of my other books listed at the bottom of this page at Amazon.

Sincerely S. G. Lee.

~0~

Books by S. G. Lee

Murder Mysteries

Love's Labour's Won
A Tiger's Heart Wrapped in a Player's Hide
Reborn – a novella~ prequel
A Penny Saved A Murder Earned
A Diller A Dollar A Really Dead Scholar
Betty Blue Lost Her Holiday Shoe
What Will Poor Robin Do?
The Kelly Murder Mysteries-Book 1-3
A Stitch in Time
Stray Bullet
Dreams Can Kill

Short Story Books
Murder Most Fowl
Jack be Nimble
Day of the Dead
Legends, Folktales and other Stories
The Stuff of Nightmares
ObsessionX2

Christmas
Christmas is Calling
The Christmas Card
The Christmas Angel
Visions of Sugarplums

Poetry
A Poetic Touch - The Human Condition

~0~

S. G. Lee